The Adventures Of The Summerswill

Leah,

Life is an amazing thing in that it doesn't stop to let you admire the speed and tenacity with which it passes. My only advice is to love each day in the way that you will fondly remember.

'The most beautiful thing, I think, is the inability of the human mind to coorelate all of its contents.'

- H.P. Lovecraft

'For We are not the giant men.'

- Timothy Lambesis

Chin up, fight for it.

- Love,

Tayla

The Adventures Of The Summerswill

Book I: Aloft
A Children's Story

by

Taylor R. Powers

Library of Congress Control Number:		2012914656
ISBN:	Hardcover	978-1-4771-5857-9
	Softcover	978-1-4771-5856-2
	Ebook	978-1-4771-5858-6

This is a work of fiction. Names, characters, places and incidents either are the product of the author's imagination or are used fictitiously, and any resemblance to any actual persons, living or dead, events, or locales is entirely coincidental.

This book was printed in the United States of America.

To order additional copies of this book, contact:
Xlibris Corporation
1-888-795-4274
www.Xlibris.com
Orders@Xlibris.com
119228

The author would like to thank the following:

My parents for all of their support and leniency while I was growing up, which allowed me to spend more time imagining. Stacey and Ally for always sticking by Timmon's side. Vaughan for appreciating the idea of a goose named Southwinter, and Olivia for believing that this book was possible. My uncle Jamie, thank you. Jason, Kristoff, Jerry, Scott, and all the rest, thanks for always believing in my art. The staff at CVAPC who always covered for me when I needed a day to write. Folger's Coffee. All of my teachers who said I couldn't make it, here you go, and for those of you who never stopped believing in me, thank you. Wal-Mart for their endless supply of low-priced movies to satiate my hunger for good cinema while I write, and for always greeting me warmly when I walk in the door. Thanks to all of the musicians out there who produce music, without having endless inspiration from songs to listen to while I write, I'd probably be lost. There are far too many of you to name. Lastly, my aunt Rosemary, Nina, and Fred Powers, thank you for everything. I am truly in your debt, you'll never know how much you've done for me.

Taylor R. Powers grew up in Cooperstown, New York, and still lives nearby. He attended the University of Massachusetts Amherst for veterinary and animal science and currently works as a veterinary technician, wrestling coach, and tattoo artist. He spends what little time is left showing exhibition poultry, exploring new artistic mediums, driving aimlessly, and always off in his own world. The Adventures of the Summerswill is his first book.

Timmon Strongtail was no ordinary otter . . . Timmon Strongtail wanted to fly. The skies above Sylva are no longer free but under the heel of a vicious Wolf. Timmon will assemble his crew and attempt to live out the stories and fables that he learned by heart as a pup. A buccaneer adventure aboard airships beginning, as all the creatures and undesireables of Sylva gather for one final battle.

The Setting Sea
High Rock
The Foothills
The Dark Forest
The Carrion Perch
N
Crow Call Falls
The Crag

High Rock
The Eyrepeak
The Autumn Woods
The Dark Forest
The Foothills
The Carrion Perch
The Owl's Eye
Crow Call Falls
The Crag

It is well-known in the Valleys of the land of Sylva that an otter's life is bound to the water. He is born among the reeds and rushes of the shore and learns to swim long before he learns to walk. He spends his life manning the skiffs and pole boats that he and his brethren use to navigate the waters of the streams and rivers and lakes of the Valleys. He rarely sets foot very far inland and spends his days baking under the noonday sun with a deck beneath his feet and spends his nights nestled in a shipboard hammock, swaying gently in the breeze, or by a campfire ashore, though never out of sight of the water. This is how all otters have lived since before time could be remembered; and seldom, if never, was it questioned.

Timmon Strongtail was no ordinary otter.

Timmon Strongtail spent his nights dreaming and most of his days daydreaming. He dreamed of the vastness of the skies, of looking down on the world as birds do, and of wind rushing through his fur as he chased his dreams westward into the setting of the sun. He grew up on his grandfather's stories of dueling sky pirates and great flying galleass and frigates, airships with wings and great fish fin-shaped keels, firing cannon at one another locked in furious battle among the clouds. He heard stories of the eagles and how they had kept the skies a safe place for all before they had left the Valleys for the lifting of warmer winds, though Timmon did not know where that was or what that meant. But the truth was . . .

. . . Timmon Strongtail wanted to fly.

"Your dreams are silly things, Tim," his father would often scold. "They are useless to you. Your family, Tim, it is your family you must think of. Who will pole the longboat when I am gone? Who will see that the pups are fed with fish from the streams? Who will call them to rise in the mornings and to supper in the evenings? No, Tim. You must think of your future, not of these silly dreams."

Timmon spent his evenings by the fireside, listening to the stories his grandfather told. The aged otter told him of fantastic times long passed when creatures sailed the skies. He told Tim of days when airships of a million colors passed overhead as frequently as the sun did and fueled Timmon's dreams.

When he had been born among the rushes, the only otter pup in his litter, Timmon Strongtail's grandfather, Miter, has woven a long white eagle feather into his fur so that it hung above his eyes and blew in the wind when Timmon ran or swam very quickly. Timmon had never removed the feather from his fur; it was by far his most prized possession.

Some evenings, when Tim was alone, he would go ashore and find a quiet place. This was often a small grove of trees, and here he would spend hours searching for the perfect weapon. He would scour the forest floor looking long and hard for a branch that was just the right length, that was straight and true, and, above all, that he could believe was the war sword of a true hero.

It was on one of these fateful evenings that Tim found himself in the middle of a grove of oak and ash and yew. He stood atop a thick fallen log, dancing this way and that, lashing out with a long wispy branch at imaginary foes. Around and around he turned, lashing out this way and that with his wooden rapier, vanquishing foe after foe until he woefully lost his footing on the moss-covered log and tumbled head over heels to the forest floor below.

"Heh, heh, heh" came a voice from among the trees, not mockingly laughing, but laughing nonetheless. Timmon could feel hot tears of embarrassments welling up in his eyes and beginning to run down his cheeks.

"Oh, come now, Tim. I meant no harm." His aged grandfather, Miter, emerged from the grove of oak and ash and yew, leaning heavily on his old blackwood staff and limping painfully with every step from an old wound that bothered him to this day.

"Hello, Grandfather."

"Hello, Tim, and might I ask who you are this day?"

"I'm Darrion Silverwing! The greatest warrior in all the skies!" Timmon thrust his wooden sword into the air triumphantly.

"Ah, a fine warrior and true then, and who are you battling that troubles you so?"

"The terrible pirates of the White-Eyed Wolf, Grandfather. They've taken the squirrel princess, Tyanna, hostage!"

"Dear me, my boy. That is quite the story. Do you remember me telling it to you when you were a pup?"

"I do, Grandfather, I always do."

"Do you know that there is much truth in that story?" Timmon cocked his head, wondering. He thought that it had just been a simple bedtime story, but could there be truth in it?

"I didn't know that, Grandfather, why didn't you tell me?"

"Oh, well, young otters enjoy stories as much as us elders. Only we elders tend to leave much of the storytelling up to a pup's imagination. I was there, you know."

Timmon could not believe his ears. "You were?"

"Yes, Tim, come sit with an old otter a moment." Miter curled his tail around his feet and groaned with age as he lowered himself onto the great log in the middle of the clearing. Tim, sheathing his wooden sword in his belt loop, trotted over and sat next to his grandfather, wrapping his own tail about his own feet, thinking that it must be a very dignified thing to do if so old an otter was doing it.

Looking up at the canopy of trees and the dying sunlight knifing through them like a thousand ribbons of orange and red, Miter Strongtail sighed deeply, clutching his blackwood staff a little closer as he did so. "Long ago, lad, the skies were full of ships. Great airships of a thousand brilliantly painted colors. Their air balloons and sails and wings were a patchwork quilt that rivaled the stuff of dreams, and they filled the skies with fantastic color. Lads like you grew up dreaming of sailing the skies, free and unencumbered. But all of this was before the White-Eyed Wolf came."

"I know this story, Grandfather, you told it to me many times. The White-Eyed Wolf came on his great black barge and drove the Eagles from the skies right?"

"No, no, no, Tim. The Eagles were not altogether driven away. No, a good many of them simply left the Valleys for the lifting of warmer winds. Those who stayed were far too few to keep the skies their own, and the other ships were never a match for the White-Eyed Wolf's Sky-skinner."

"Why did the Eagles leave, Grandfather?"

"I never knew, Tim. One of mine own oldest friends, one of the truest warriors I ever knew was with me when I took the wound that still vexes me so, and he was one of the last to stay. You wear his feather in your hair, lad." Miter plucked knowingly at the eagle feather braided into Timmon's fur, and it danced a little in a quiet breeze that ruffled the leaves of the oak and ash and yew trees around them.

"Who was he?"

"Prettle Snowhelm, the greatest eagle I ever knew, and a true friend."

"What happened to him?" Timmon shifted a little on the log, inching closer to hear more.

"Oh, lad. I never saw him again after that day. He saved my life, you know? I took only this small wound in mine own leg, though painful it still is."

"You were a pirate?"

"Oh, heavens no, lad! We styled ourselves buccaneers. We sailed the skies in the good and honest way that only those who have seen the ends of the world can know. We reached the ends of the land where only water can be seen, where the sun drowns itself each day only to be reborn in the east. I have seen the great north where it is always autumn and cold and the deep south where it rains every day and the water from the skies is warm as a bath. And I have been again to the east to see where the sun rises each day. I have seen this world, Tim, and I am grateful for it." Timmon Strongtail's eyes were full of wonder, dazzled at the sights playing out in his imagination. "Your father tells me that you dream too, not just of greater things than this old river we plod back and forth day after day and year after year, but of seeing the skies and the world beneath you?"

"I do, Grandfather."

"Then I give you this." Miter Strongtail hefted his blackwood staff as though it were light as a feather and passed it knowingly into the paws of his wide-eyed grandson. Timmon was not sure whether his eyes were deceiving him, but he looked closer than he ever had before at the staff in his hands and realized for the first time that it was not simply black, as blackwood is, but that it danced with a thousand carvings all in heart-of-gold.

"It's carved, Grandfather. Why, I can see you in it! I see me on this log! And there's Darrion Silverwing! All the stories of old, Grandfather. How did you carve all of this?"

"I didn't, Tim. There is much you must learn, and this is the best way that I have to teach you. Remember always that blackwood never forgets a hand that touches it nor a story it overhears. Few trees do, they all remember."

"Where did you get this?"

"This staff was given to me by mine own grandfather, and to him by his, for many generations. But long ago, it was carved by an ancient seer, one who was known to speak to the trees themselves. He wrought this staff of blackwood because it is the oldest of all the trees, each one growing since before creatures walked the Valleys. In it, he inlaid heart-of-gold with the knowledge that the staff would remember all it ever heard or felt or received through the touch of one worthy enough to wield it, for you see, trees never forget. Take this with you, Tim, it is the dearest thing I possess. You remind me of myself as a young pup, more than you will ever know, full of dreams and wonder. Alas, I cannot go with you, but with this, I shall never be far from your side, and it shall teach you all you need to know on your journey."

"Journey?"

"I'm letting you go, Tim. You must go and live your dreams. Set out on the road west toward the setting sun, follow it through the forest until you arrive at the foothills of a great mountain; there you will find an inn called the Rising Sun. Seek out Wattle Featherscarf, for he is the finest captain that I ever sailed under or knew. There too you will meet Teera Proudleap; let her guide you on your way, for she is also wise. And remember, Tim, as long as you go on your adventure with wind in your hair and love in your heart, you will never want for fulfillment. Because a full heart is a full soul, and your heart has more to give than you know."

Timmon left his family's longboat by way of a small hatch at the aft side. Blackwood staff with all of his belongings hefted over his shoulder, he hopped the railing of the deck and landed with a small splash amid the rushes and cattails of the riverbank. It was pure dark outside the warmth and lamplight of the longboat's interior, and it took Timmon's eyes a few moments to adjust to the night, and there was very little light from the sliver of moon overhead to aid his way. The young otter turned and, for a minute, looked back at the life he was leaving behind, the simplicity of a life navigating the rivers of the valley. Of fishing for each supper and charting course by way of maps that had been in the family for generations, of simply finding proper moorings each evening to put to anchor and wait for the coming of the sun each morning, he did not regret leaving and, with a hefty sigh, realized that his only regret was leaving behind a family that, despite their insistence on his being tied down, loved him very much. He would miss them dearly but realized that he would return to visit when he was a famous buccaneer and that a caged bird must always long to fly. He turned on his heel in the shallow waters and strode off into the darkness, west toward the lands where the sun set.

"What beast that embraces two halves of this entire world, is nestled 'twixt hard tail and wing unfurled? Whence the sun hast cracked her rays to splinters, opposite snakes whose scales harden in winters. O'er the consumption of all is her birth, to all new things of all new worth."

These cryptic words had been the last things that Miter Strongtail had muttered to Timmon, moments before Tim had left the boat, and had stopped only briefly to the family room where his grandfather slumbered by the fire. Lightly touching his grandfather's sleeping paw, he was startled when his grandfather had grasped his own paw and uttered these phrases, half in and half out of one of his deep and long naps by the fireside. Timmon had tried to commit them to memory but was having trouble keeping all the words straight, and he instead stumbled on into the darkness of the west, onward on his journey.

It was only an hour or two before Timmon was certain that he was good and lost. He had walked straight as he could westward, but it had only been minutes into the forest when he had began to doubt himself. He heard strange sounds emanate from the woods around him, haunting calls and faraway shrieks. He felt he saw eyes all around him and felt watched from all sides. Each time he felt he caught a glimpse of a strange creature, he would turn to confront it, again and again until he was very surely turned around, and in the pitch dark of the forest, realized he could no longer tell what direction he was facing. He found himself in the center of a thick stand of trees; and frustrated and near tears, he sat down on a large rock and wrapped his tail around his feet, clutching his blackwood staff close, taking comfort from it.

It was a moment before he noticed the shifting and fluttering of the heart-of-gold inlay in the blackwood staff. Like curls of smoke, the symbols, shapes, and pictures began to rewrite themselves.

Timmon was at first perplexed, and even a little frightened, until he remembered his grandfather's words, It shall teach you all you need to know . . .

Gathering the staff before his eyes, Timmon stared intently at the pictures taking shape before him. Slowly, wrought in gold, a definite image began to take shape, a boulder, bearded in moss on one side. Swirling around the boulder, in carved finery a snowflake, then another, and soon a flurry of gusting snow that hovered around the moss-bearded end of the boulder that had not been there moments before.

Timmon gathered himself and thought as clearly as he could. A gust of snow toward the mossy side of a boulder? Presently he realized exaltedly that he was, himself, seated on a large stone. He leaped into the air and ran all around the stone, feeling with his paw until he found that one side was soft with the growth of moss and that no other side could boast the same charge. If that were so, then perhaps the snow meant a direction? He was lost after all. Snow was cold and flew south in the winter from the northern skies, north! He then remembered something his father had told him when he was still a much-smaller pup, that whenever he turned around on a river, he could gather direction by seeking out a shore-side rock and finding the side of the stone that held the most moss, and this would surely always be north. Bouncing with excitement, Timmon put the mossy side of the boulder behind him and swiftly turned to his right, straight west.

With a newfound skip in his step, Timmon set off into the night once more, holding tightly to the blackwood staff as he had not before, more truly understanding the importance of it and the love and wisdom bestowed upon him by his grandfather by its gift.

"What beast that embraces two halves of this world whole."

Within the course of several hours of walking through the darkness, guided by his blackwood staff, Timmon found that he had grown quite tired. He came upon an open grove of birch trees, all in a circle, and at its center, a thick patch of moss, soft as any bed.

Timmon settled down and curled his tail about his feet, removing a small hunk of hard bread from the bindle tied to his staff. He chewed on the bread thoughtfully, taking in the darkness of his surroundings, though his eyes had long ago adjusted to the night. The birch trees were silver in their splendor and looked less like bones and more like the stripes of moonlight that laid themselves out on a new harbor with each moment. Timmon was less and less afraid and soon lost himself to a dreamless sleep.

Timmon's eyes snapped open; he had been asleep for what felt like only moments but what was closer to an hour. The hunk of hard bread that had been in his hand when he had fallen asleep had disappeared entirely, and he could not remember eating the rest of it, and this made him very nervous. Hackles raised he clutched his staff, looking about in the night for the presence of another creature. It took only a moment for Timmon to realize that he was not indeed alone. He sensed something looking on him and looked all about for a flash of eyes in the wan moonlight.

"Who's there?" His voice was little more than a whisper in his fear.

"Hoo, indeed?" came the answer, lilting and from high above him.

"Show yourself!" Timmon brandished his staff with all the resolve he could muster, but it was weighted wrong because of the bindle tied to its end and felt clumsy in his hands.

"First might I comment on the rudeness of coming into another's grove, sleeping without permission, and then brandishing what appears to be a weapon with such gall? It's quite improper of a guest, especially one who comes in the middle of the night. Though night and day I fear are somewhat complicated concepts for me to waylay onto another creature not of mine own type. I do however thank you for the hard bread."

"You . . . you ate my bread?"

"Oh, indeed. It seemed you were finished with your meal, and it having been a particularly poor night of meal-getting for myself, I helped myself. If anything, I took what was offered by an intruder into mine own grove, and helped you seem a more polite guest."

Timmon looked all around and still could not discern the direction from which the voice was coming. He held his staff a little higher, hoping to perhaps see a little farther by the light of the heart-of-gold inlay wrought into it. "Sh-show yourself."

"I might have hoped for a more polite way of request. But I suppose . . ." A great black shape descended from the birch trees above, its size betrayed only by the moonlight it eclipsed, for it made not a sound. Before Timmon sat the largest owl he had ever seen. It was twice his height, with feathers that shone bronze and silver and the deepest copper in the light of his staff. Its eyes were great molten orbs as large as Timmon's head, and its great head was topped with two curling tufts of feathers that looked in the shifting light like horns. Beneath his grand beak was a tuft of pearly white feathers, not unlike the snow-white beard his grandfather wore, and Timmon thought that this owl must be quite old. His talons were covered with silver feathers, thought they were hooked wickedly and as dark as the deepest river depths. He wore a brass monocle with a long chain that hung to his waist, which was adorned with a thick sash that hung with a menagerie of herbs and stoppered bottles and several bundles wrapped in cloth. "May I have the pleasure of introducing myself, lad? I am Hoory Softflight. And this is my grove, though admittedly it has only been so for a fortnight or so. I am myself something of a wanderer, and I go whence I am needed often as not. And you are?"

"T-T-Timmon Strongtail." Timmon was at quite a loss for words at the appearance of this large creature and found himself scrambling to find the right thing to say. "I-I-I apologize for trespassing on your grove, Mr. Softflight."

"Oh, please. I admit I was somewhat harsh at first, but I did help myself to your hard bread when no permission was formally asked. Let us let bygones be bygones? In truth, one cannot claim to own the forest in its entirety, so how can one claim to own a couple trees? And please, dear lad, call me Hoory. I prefer mine own name that my mother gave me whence I hatched to the titles bestowed upon me."

"Titles?"

"Oh, mister, doctor, philosopher, and the like. I'm an owl of many talents, lad. Which brings me to your own title. May I call you Timmon?"

"Of course." Timmon found himself somewhat disarmed by the owl's kindness and finally lowered his blackwood staff to his side, unconsciously lowering his hackles; at the same time, he extended his paw in way of formal greeting. Hoory Softflight said simply, "Pleased to meet you, Timmon." And he extended a few primary feathers, which Timmon shook carefully, not wanting to ruffle them.

"Might I ask what one so young is doing this deep in the forest at this time of night?"

"I am walking west. I'm to find an Admiral Featherscarf at the Inn of the Rising Sun. I mean to be a buccaneer."

"A buccaneer is it? Well, surely, lad, you know there have been no buccaneers in the sky since the Eagles left the Valleys for the lifting of warmer winds?"

"I know, Mr. Softflight."

"Hoory, please."

"I know, Hoory. I mean to be the first." Timmon puffed out his chest and arched his neck in what he hoped cut an imposing figure.

"Well, lad, if you hope to take on the White-Eyed Wolf alone, then I name you fool. But if you're going west, then I suppose you'd like some company?"

"Company?" Timmon was not sure what to make of the owl's offer. "But can't you only travel at night?"

"Don't otters only travel by day? You seem to have come a long way in the dark of night, lad."

"To be sure, would you like to come with me, Hoory?"

"I shall travel with you as far as the inn, I suppose, and then we'll have to see. The way you talk of this journey it seems as if you have a long way to go yet."

"I suppose I do." Timmon was quite struck then by how far he was from home and how far he still had yet to go.

"Well, lad, any journey is much better met when with friends. Agreed?"

Timmon lit up at the idea. "Yes, yes, I suppose it is."

"Shall we be off then, are you rested?" Hoory turned a little on his feathered talons as if to make off west.

"I am." The truth was Timmon felt more invigorated than he had since seated on a log with his grandfather, now that he had a friend to make the journey with. Together an aged owl and a young otter set off on foot into the darkness of the night, and toward the west, the first light of the rising sun just peeking over the horizon to their backs cutting the forest into shades of lightning grays and spearheads of morning yellow and gold.

"Is nestled 'twixt hard tail and wing unfurled."

"Tum-te-tum-te-tee!" Hoory hooted as the two adventurers ambled along. It was midmorning, and though the sun had not reached its pinnacle in the sky, the forest was alight with colors and sounds. The rays of golden-white light cut swathes through the vermillion leaves, and there was not a cloud to be seen to obscure the deepest azure of the sky through the canopy. Their path was now as sure as ever as it was clear the direction they traveled by the sun, and their pace had not slowed since they had left before dawn.

"How much farther, Hoory?" Timmon asked, trying not to sound inappreciative or like he was whining.

"Oh, I imagine we'll walk the rest of today and perhaps most of tomorrow at the least. Were you a smaller creature I might just have you climb aboard so we could fly there. Alas, you're just a might too grown for me."

"I should have liked that."

"Oh, you'll be flying soon enough, correct? Once we meet Admiral Featherscarf and find you a suitable means of conveyance."

"Do you know the admiral, Hoory?" Timmon could not help but imagine a great eagle, resplendent with a chestful of old medals and stripes of honor, perhaps gilded in armor.

"Indeed I have met him a few times in passing, mostly at the Inn of the Rising Sun if truth be told. He is a fine bird, though if I may be candid, I believe he thinks the glory days of buccaneers have long passed him by. He mumbles often of the great loss that the Valleys suffered when the Eagles left for the lifting of warmer winds. He is hope-scorned, though may still yet be a powerful ally, and I think your grandfather was wise in sending you to seek his consul."

"My grandfather sailed the skies with him, and he said that he was the finest admiral that he ever sailed under."

"In his day, he was. Though he is an aged bird now, Tim." Timmon's heart sank a little, and he slumped his shoulders. "Oh, but I didn't mean to spurn your hope, Tim! I only meant that he may take some convincing. Or maybe none at all, come to think, it's been such a long time since I spoke with the good admiral."

"Then there's hope?"

"Oh, there's always hope, lad. For anything, any day, the world is an amazing place after all." Timmon reflected on this and thought to ask.

"Hoory, have you ever seen one of these before?" He held up his heart-of-gold inlaid blackwood staff for Hoory to look closely at while they walked.

"I have hazarded a glance or two at your fine stick while we've walked, Tim, and I can honestly say it is the only one I have ever seen like it. Whence did you come by it?"

"It was my grandfather's," Timmon said proudly, holding the staff with something not unlike tenderness. "He gave it to me when I set out last night. It remembers."

"Oh, all trees remember, Timmon. All trees and roots and branches and twigs and sticks and leaves remember everything they have ever seen or felt. But it is a very special stick indeed that can show you its wisdom. You have quite a treasure there."

"It isn't a stick."

"It is a stick. A very nice stick. Until you learn to wield it like a staff, it will always be a stick. And I know just the way to show you otherwise."

"You do?"

"Well, not me personally." Hoory chuckled and muffed his feathers. "But I know just the lass, and we'll be meeting her at the inn if I can gauge correctly. Well, she's there often as not in any case. Healing I can teach you, combat is another matter."

"I see." Timmon looked down at the blackwood staff in his paws, fondly, watching the heart-of-gold inlay play across it in scenes of elaborate beauty. "It's not a stick."

"Tum-te-tum-te-tee!"

Sometime nearer the onset of evening, Hoory and Timmon came upon a small stream, gurgling almost happily with clear water over round, worn stones, with shores thick with reeds and cattails.

"Shall we rest here for the night, lad?" Hoory asked, stretching his wings high above his head. "I daresay I've tired myself out with all this walking."

"I suppose. Do you think we could sleep there?" Timmon indicated a small spot beneath a mammoth-weeping willow, where a curve of stream formed a deep limpid pool that glowed pink with the dying daylight.

"I believe that that would be a capital place to rest for the evening. Perhaps you could fetch us some dry wood for a small fire. I'll see what I can scrounge from the forest for a small supper."

Timmon liked the idea and set about gathering up some kindling while Hoory strode off into the forest searching among the underbrush for berries and fruit.

Before too long, Timmon had a growing pile of dry branches, twigs, and grass. He took a pair of flint stones from the bindle on his blackwood staff. Holding one in each of palm of his paw he struck stone against stone several times until sparks flew to a small bundle of grass at the center of the pyre, catching their red embers and igniting ever so slightly.

It was not long before Hoory returned with a wingful of berries, roots, and nuts.

"Now, Tim, let the fire die down to embers and then form a small divot with them like this." Hoory took a small branch from a nearby tree and formed a small indent in the glowing coals beneath the fire and piled it full of nuts, covering it again with more coal and embers. "They'll roast nice and soft now. You'll really be able to taste the flavor. Now do we have a pot?"

"A pot?" Timmon rummaged through the bindle tied to his blackwood staff and produced a small metal bowl with a handle.

"Ah, brilliant!" With great dexterity and speed, Hoory erected a small dutch oven out of nearby branches and drew some water from the limpid pool, placing the roots in the bowl, and letting them boil over the flames. "Now horseradish and leeks may be a little pungent for your taste, but I find them delightful. Have some berries." Hoory extended a wingful of berries to Timmon. "Blackberries, raspberries, and gooseberries, it's quite amazing what the forest herself can provide when a creature is in need."

Timmon took the berries in his paws and ate a few gingerly at first, then, realizing his appetite was properly whetted, buried his face in his paws and devoured the remainder of the berries hastily.

"Undignified but acceptable all the same." Hoory watched the pot of leeks and horseradish closely and stirred the roasting nuts with a branch pensively.

"I'm sorry, just hungry is all," Timmon mumbled, wiping berry juice from his chin with the back of his paw.

"No, no, it's quite all right, you've come a long way, lad. You must be famished. I'm only happy I could find you something to eat, and you've done a fine job erecting this fire here."

"My grandfather taught me how to tent the branches and make a flue. I owe it to him, I owe a lot to him."

"He sounds to be quite the figure of wisdom in your life. Pity I never knew him."

"You'll meet him someday after we've left for the skies." Timmon looked longingly up at the stars above them and then back to the warmth and blaze of the fire before him.

"Might I ask you something, Tim?"

"Of course, Mr. Softflight."

"Hoory, please. Your feather? From whence did it come?"

Timmon fingered the eagle feather woven into his fur just above his eyes, "This? This was a gift from my grandfather. It belonged to an eagle that he knew when they both sailed the skies. Prettle Snowhelm was his name?"

"Ah, truly? The last eagle. I know of that warrior."

"What do you mean? You did know him?"

"I did. He was the last eagle to stay in the Valleys after all the others left for the lifting of warmer and kinder winds. He was as true a soul as I ever knew."

"What happened to him?"

Hoory looked deeply inside himself and thought of what to say. "The truth is, lad the White-Eyed Wolf took his life in the last stand of all the sky-faring creatures against him."

"When was that?"

"Oh, a long time ago now. As I understand, your grandfather may have been there, as he knew him well. Lad, do you realize what it means that you're on this quest?"

"What do you mean?" Timmon's spirit dropped some then, and he clutched his blackwood staff close for comfort and wrapped his tail around his feet.

"Do you know what it means to be a skinner, lad? An animal, any animal, any creature under our sun that rises in the east and submerges itself 'neath the sea in the west is sacred. We are as sacred in life as we are in death. And to take an animal's life, and then to"—Hoory paused, unsure of whether to go on—"t-t-to skin them, lad, is the most grievous of offenses. This wolf wears a skin at all times. A great arctic bear fought him for his life long ago. When the White-Eyed Wolf took his life, he also took his skin." Timmon was quite horrified by this point and hugged himself with his arms, afraid.

"Even his great airship bears the name of his atrocity. The Sky-Skinner, it is called. He is as horrible and terrible a foe as any could want. I do not mean to frighten you, lad, only to invoke in you an understanding of the magnitude of what you wish to do. Do you understand?"

"I do. As awful a creature as he may be, I am not afraid." Though Timmon was quite afraid at this point. "I want to be the one to free the skies from him."

"Then you will need good friends at your side, lad. If you'll have me, I would like to be one of them."

"You would?" Timmon was speechless with anticipation.

"Indeed. I said I'd come as far as the Inn of the Rising Sun, though after thinking about it, I've quite decided that my life is growing long, but I believe there is time enough for one last adventure, time to do something more. I'm with you, lad, as far as you wish to go."

Tears welled in Timmon's eyes, and he quickly wiped them away, not wanting to seem too emotional, though his heart had swelled with the presence of such a good friend met in so short a time.

"Then we continue on in the morning," Timmon said, standing and holding his blackwood staff as imposingly as he could, as he thought a true warrior should.

Hoory was instantly distracted by a small pop and a crack from the embers of the fire and fished a nut out of the coals and popped it in his beak, cracking the shell and sucking down its contents quickly, "The nuts are done!"

"Opposite snakes whose scales harden in winters."

Timmon attempted again and again to commit his grandfather's words to memory but soon found his eyelids feeling heavy as stone, and he could not help but drift off to a deep sleep.

Timmon dreamed that night of home. In his sleep he saw the glowing red and golden hearth fire of their cabin beneath the deck of the family's longboat. Around it sat his father, his grandfather, who looked much younger than when last Timmon had seen him, his mother, and a bouncing otter pup that he thought must be himself.

Through the cabin window he could see that the first snows of winter had begun to dance and swirl through the darkness outside, like a million stars against a blanket of opal sky, moving to the tune of a quick ballad that no one could hear. Similarly, his father and grandfather were telling a story, like they used to when Timmon had been only a pup. His grandfather would paint a verbal picture of wonderful fantasies and heroic tales, only to be interjected at inopportune moments by his father's insipid comments, often cutting down the true wonder of the story with realistic observations and short-sighted quips. Despite this familiar scene, Timmon could no more hear his family or their story than he could hear the celestial song of the snow.

The closer Timmon tried to edge his way along a dark and invisible precipice toward his family, the further he seemed to slip along an unknown and unfelt slope. The harder he struggled, pushing with his tail and digging all four paws into the ground, the further he seemed to slip away.

A great figure rose between him, and his vision then, a figure as dark as any night Timmon had ever witnessed, swathed in a brilliant ivory fur about its massive shoulders. A single star-white eye gleamed from beneath a furrowed onyx brow. The single eye was soon joined by a crescent grin of too-many teeth to fill any creature's mouth, gleaming like pearl razors and dripping saliva in rivers.

Timmon screamed then, afraid, and found that he had jolted himself awake. Sweat stuck to his fur all over, and he found himself blindly grasping for his blackwood staff, finding it, and clutching it close to his breast.

"Bad dream?" Hoory rolled slightly onto one shoulder to look at Tim with his great golden eyes, full of concern.

"Y-Y-Yes. Sorry I woke you, Hoory."

"Think nothing of it." Hoory rolled back onto his back, absentmindedly poking at the dying embers of the fire with a stick, stirring them. "You know, Tim, all creatures feel fear. I have met every sort of animal in this world, and the one thing they all have in common is fear. A serpent may never hold a grudge, and a bear may never feel jealousy of another, and a robin may never long for home again once he's left the nest, but the great equalizer is fear. No matter the size or ferociousness, all creatures at some point feel fear. And there is no shame in that, ever. Because even the greatest adventurers often feel a little afraid before they set off. Remember that." With that Hoory closed his eyes and was asleep in moments, hooting snores beneath the weeping willow where they had made their camp.

Timmon, a little reassured, held his blackwood staff closer to his chest where it glowed softly in a rhythm in tune with Timmon's heartbeat, closed his eyes, and tried desperately to forget the vision his dreams had brought him and fall back to sleep. He tried to be as brave as he could.

The next morning, Timmon and Hoory broke camp and set out to the west before the sun's golden eyelid had barely cracked over the purple rim of the horizon. By now, the deep forest had begun to recede behind them as they entered the lower foothills, rolling knolls covered in scrub brush and spike-grass. The occasional trees that could be seen were spindly and often thin of leaf.

By midmorning, Timmon and Hoory found themselves in the cusp of three very tall knolls, one to their left, one to their right, and the tallest of the three rising directly before them, a precipitous shale bank grown over sparsely with tiny blue flowers and intermittent shocks of grasses.

Betwixt the three knolls was a small pool of water, clear as undisturbed thought, and full at the bottom with smooth round stones of a thousand shades of blue and gray.

"We ought to rest here for a few minutes, Tim. Our journey is nearing its end, or perhaps its beginning, depending on how you view the situation, I suppose."

"What do you mean, Hoory?" Timmon settled on a boulder the perfect size for a seat, crooked his blackwood staff under his arm, and curled his tail about his feet, letting its tip dangle in the water a little, whisking it this way and that, causing concentric ripples that dazzled in the midmorning sun.

"Well," said Hoory as he plopped himself down, rather unceremoniously on a small outcrop of shale, "the Inn of the Rising Sun is quite near now. If you look overhead you should just be able to spot the peak of the mountain it rests under over the top of that knoll there."

Timmon craned his neck to look and could indeed see a cloudy fish fin of faraway stone rising high into the sky, cloaked in swirling clouds, and blanketed in snow that reflected the golden light of the sun so well that it simply glowed like a torch itself.

"It's quite beautiful, Hoory."

"Indeed it is. That is the Eyriepeak, whence the eagles once roosted and nested. The mists that surround it make it almost ethereal in most sunlight or moonlight, such that it took many years for the White-Eyed Wolf to ever discover it."

"Is it then, h-h-his home now?" Timmon asked with more than a little quiver in his voice.

"Oh, heavens no, Tim. The Eyriepeak is far too steep or treacherous for any airship to simply dock there or even to make a proper landing atop. Indeed it is too tall for even the most tenacious of songbirds to attempt to fly to safely. The eagles in their day were in fact the only creatures who could safely call that mountain their home, and I suppose that is why they did so. No, Tim, nowadays the Eyriepeak is home to none."

"Have you ever been up there, Hoory?" Timmon looked wide-eyed at the precipitous golden peak that rose above the horizon just beyond his focused vision, like some great sail out of a dream, carried by an unseen wind into the realm of reality.

"No, Timmon, I'm afraid not. When the eagles occupied the Eyriepeak, it was the most grievous of insults to simply invite oneself in, like making a grove as one's own bedplace without first asking the permission of the current occupant." Hoory added with a quiet smirk, a wink, and a barely audible chuckle, and upon seeing Timmon lower his head in noticeable shame, quickly added, "Oh, but I jest, Tim. It was a poor joke. I apologize. But in answer to your question more definitively, no, I have never been to the Eryiepeak."

"I see. And how far did you say we are from the Inn of the Rising Sun, Hoory?"

"Oh, it's just over that rise. Surely if you could climb that knoll you'd be able to see it quite clear." Hoory barely finished his sentence before Timmon had snatched up his blackwood staff, bounded through the pool at which they sat, making quite a show of splashing water all around, and began scrambling up the shale bank toward the west on all fours as fast as he could manage. When Timmon had reached the peak of the knoll, he gasped in awe at the first sight to greet him, holding on to his blackwood staff for support, for his knees quite gave way under him, and without it he would certainly have collapsed.

There in the distance, Timmon saw for the fist time, the triangular multicolored sails and deep red hull, complete with a spearlike foremast, and rising splendor of a cabin building at the bulkhead, fin-shaped starboard and port sails and a great arched rudder . . .

. . . of an airship.

"Ah, the Inn of the Rising Sun." Hoory crested the knoll shortly after and found Timmon staring in disbelief at the airship grounded atop a grassy hill.

"The Inn? But, Hoory?" Timmon rubbed his eyes, perplexed, looking again and again at the massive sky-faring vessel some distance away.

"Yes, Tim?"

"It's an airship, isn't it?" Timmon again rubbed his eyes with his paws, cocked his head to one side, still wondering if his eyes had tricked him in some way.

"Indeed, lad. That is the Summerswill. Once the finest galley in the Greenfleet, under the captainship of Admiral Wattle Featherscarf. She was grounded many years ago, and since has been known as the Inn of the Rising Sun, it's there that we will procure your crew, and your vessel if I do not overstep in assuming she still flies."

"If?"

"Well, assuming we can still decipher the ship's lock, or that the admiral still remembers the key to making her sky-worthy."

"You're speaking in circles, Hoory." Timmon folded his arms. He was not sure whether he was disappointed. He had come so far, and the first airship Timmon had laid eyes on was grounded; its sails were limp with lack of wind; her hull now appeared soil-stained with disuse and the finlike starboard and port sails, in his dreams it had been the powerful wings of an eagle, and now it seemed more like the waterlogged and flimsy appendages of a raven caught in a hurricane.

"I suppose I am, though it shall be made clear whence we have made contact with the creatures within. They know far more regarding sky sailing and buccaneering than I ever shall. Come, let us finish this portion of your journey." Hoory straightened his monocle and set off down the knoll.

Timmon shouldered his blackwood staff and bindle, walking carefully down the slope with a little less skip in his step, and slightly disheartened, failed to notice the soft luminescent glow of his blackwood staff that hummed and throbbed, its heart or gold carvings swirling like smoke and dancing in and out of ethereal images, faster and faster as they approached the long-moored Summerswill.

A large circular door had been carved in the deep-red hull of the Summerswill; in its center a circular window spilled warm, golden light out into the late-afternoon day. Steam or smoke, fragrant nonetheless, spilled beyond the cracks of the door's edges in small tangled tendrils. A hodge-podge sign had been erected to the left of the pathway leading to the front door, advertising this moored airship as the Inn of the Rising Sun, and had been cut into the shape of a bright-yellow orb, encircled by radically apexed pyramids of red and orange and white and yellow and bright pink.

Timmon and Hoory, walking side by side, had barely reached the door before it burst open into the day, the light inside eclipsed entirely by a massive figure as the sun by the moon.

"Look 'er out!" The figure brought up a pair of thickly muscled green-brown arms, capped by thousand-times-stained oven mitts, hefting a massive pot of what looked to be old stew. Not looking around in any fashion, the figure thrust the pot to the end of his arms reach and quickly pulled it back, causing a thick curdled wall of old soup and bits of vegetable and sodden bread to fly willy-nilly out the door . . .

. . . and straight at Timmon Strongtail's wide-eyed surprised face.

Tepid broth, sliced carrots, zucchini, turnips, potatoes, leeks and onions, hunks of hard bread, now squishy and sodden with soup, flurries of spices from a dozen different herbs and, finally, a massive wooden serving spoon (which had been forgotten at the bottom of the pot) catapulted into Timmon, knocking him to his backside in the dirt as he dropped his blackwood staff in a futile attempt to throw his paws before his eyes.

Hoory, spared from the soupy onslaught, hooted with joy and exclaimed, "Brattleby! So good to see you!"

The massive, muscle armed tortoise, just noticing the aged owl before him, promptly dropped his pot to the ground and embraced with his old friend.

Neither quite noticed the soup-sodden otter by their feet.

"Ah, Hoory, old friend. T's been some time, ho've you been keepin'?"

"Well, and better still my good tortoise. It's a pleasure for the soul to see you again. Might I be expecting too much to taste that famous leek and lentil stew of yours tonight?" Hoory spread his wings to their full span excitedly.

"Not at all, not at all, m' old owl. I say, I was jus' castin' out the dregs from last nigh' and . . . I say, that an otter?"

"Mm, um, oh . . . goodness yes! Timmon, are you all right?" A smidgen slighted, Timmon sat up, dredging vegetable from his fur and combing the soup from his eagle feather with a paw.

"I'm fine, just, er, soaked now, Hoory. Thank you though." Timmon managed to stand without slipping in puddled soup. Before him stood the largest tortoise Timmon had ever seen, coincidentally it was the first tortoise Timmon had ever seen. He stood a full head taller than Hoory Softflight and was seemingly forged of nothing but taught roped muscles covered almost in entirety by tattooed spirals and swirls and knot work. His eyes were heavily lidded, such that only the smallest sliver of wizened brown showed beneath. His face was lined with age though he was perhaps not as old as Timmon judged, and he wore an oven mitt on each claw, stained a thousand different colors as was the absurdly small apron he wore about his thick waist. Timmon noticed also that his shell was etched with tattoos, adding a wholly new depth to the existing patterns of red and orange that arrayed it.

"Timmon, may I have the exquisite pleasure of introducing, Brattleby Plateback, chef extraordinare," said Hoory.

Timmon extended a dripping paw, and it was met with a massive oven-mitted claw.

"A ples'r, lad. And you would be?"

"Timmon Strongtail, sir. I mean to be a buccaneer."

"A buccaneer is it? Hoory what tall tales have you been filling this young one's head wit'?"

"I assure you, Brattleby, the otter had ideas on mind when I first met him. He knew already of the inn and was headed west whence we crossed paths." Hoory laid a reassuring spread of primary feathers over Timmon's soup-soaked shoulders.

"I see. Strongtail, eh? You wouldn't, er . . . be the son o' Miter? Would you?"

"Miter Strongtail is my grandfather, sir. This should prove it," Timmon untied the bindle full of food and supplies from the head of his blackwood staff and held it forward for the tortoise to inspect. In true form, the symbols that danced across its surface began to swirl and jig, flashing brightly in heart-of-gold in the sunlight outside of the Inn of the Rising Sun.

Golden shapes and stories reflected in his deep brown eyes, Brattleby Plateback exclaimed, "Well, I'll be! 'Tis the staff o' the old otter hi'sself. Whence did you come by 'tis thing lad?"

"It was my grandfather's, good sir. He sent it with me when I set out from home nearly a week ago. I mean to sail the skies."

"Ah, yes. You've mentioned that, lad. An' that ain't a quandary I 'kin help you wit'. Though the ol' bird who can is inside this here inn. Though I'll tell you plain, he don't remember the key to the ships lock no more. Been many years since this ol' bird wasn't ground-bound." He waved an oven mitt, gesturing behind him at the hulk of the airship Summerswill, her sails hanging limp in the still air, and her hull a pale shadow of its once-magnificent self.

Timmon was a bit unnerved by what Brattleby had said but pressed on puffing his chest out boldly.

"I wish to speak with the admiral, Wattle Featherscarf. I need to consort with him regarding the crew of this ship and her preparations for her next journey."

"All righ', all righ', lad. Come on in, I'll introduce you to the admiral." Brattleby picked up his pot and ladle in his massively mitted claws and opened the round door behind him.

Steam and smoke scented like herbs and spices, and the raucous laughter of many spilled out of the open doorway with an audible wave, and Timmon for the first time glimpsed the interior of the Summerswill. The inside of the hull was the same deep red as the deck and sides, and a thousand candles peppered the beams and sconces and candelabras that hung from the ceiling. A dozen tables crowded with creatures of all shapes and sizes bustled with excitement and loud storytelling, and in the corner a massive stone heart burned bright with a cook-fire, over which hung many pots and pans all simmering with dishes that smelled simply delectable.

Between the tables strolled a pair of squirrels, one clearly older than the other, serving drinks and bowls of soups and hunks of hard bread. Both wore aprons over brilliantly colored vests, and each had any number of bangles and bells and scarves tied into their tails so that they swirled with brilliant colors and jingled as they hopped from table to table.

At the bar sat a large goose with feathers the color of bronze and white and mud. He wore a tricornered hat atop his head and was quite jowly. About his midsection he wore a thick belt stuffed to every inch with all manner of scrolls and folded papers. In his left eye he wore a loupe and was busily studying a map before him that looked quite ancient. Between sips of his drink and bites of his fruit plate he would occasionally honk obnoxiously.

"There 'e is, lad. Best go say 'ello." Brattleby indicated the far corner of the inn's dining room with one mitted claw. Timmon, who had been eyeing the goose at the bar, thinking that he might be the admiral was turned in gaze to the darkest recesses of the inn. There, beneath a single burning candle, frozen drips of years of wax hanging like mountain icicles above his head, sat a vulture.

"The admiral, is . . . is he?" Timmon stuttered some, surprised at seeing such a creature in such a place. He had never laid eyes on a vulture before, though most of the creatures he saw at that moment were indeed new to him; this one was a fearsome spectacle.

"Indeed, lad. He's a vulture." Brattleby placed an oven-mitted claw in the small of Timmon's back, leading him forward. Timmon scarcely noticed the turning heads of many of the creatures in the dining room, craning for a look at this newcomer, as his eyes were fixed on the admiral. He wore the largest hat Timmon had ever seen, a single grand feather, twice the size of Tim's, sprang from behind a crimson brooch at its front, and it was patched a dozen times with a dozen different colors. It had no discernable shape and was more an amorphous enigma than a hat in true form. He held a great walking stick that was clearly formed of taproot from the way it twisted and mangled its own form from floor to shoulder height. His head was banded with several small banners or varying color and size. About his shoulders he wore an aged dark blue jacket with golden epaulettes so faded that they appeared as white as the jacket appeared gray, this too was torn and worn in many places and patched in a very haphazard way. From his collar sprang an unkempt wreath of feathers, all askew and unruly, and from there sprouted his naked fleshy neck, wrinkled and rolled with age. His eyes were hidden beneath his very large hat, but his beak was a massive hooked thing that hung out from beneath his hat like a cliff face over an abyss. He did not speak as Timmon and Brattleby approached but merely sipped from the tankard before him on the table.

"Er, Admiral, this 'ere otter would like ta' meet you." Brattleby shoved Timmon forward a little, and Timmon was forced to catch himself with his blackwood staff posted into the floor.

Then the admiral spoke a low gruff rattling voice that cracked and splintered its way from his beak, and he cocked his head in such a way that his eyes were finally visible under his hat, and Timmon saw for the first time that they were a piercing ice-blue and seemed to stare right through him when he asked, "Where did you get that?"

His eyes were on Timmon's blackwood staff.

At the sound of the vulture's voice, many of the creatures within the Inn of the Rising Sun cocked their heads or craned their ears to listen closer; it was seldom that the old admiral, Wattle Featherscarf gave voice to thought.

Timmon clutched his staff close to his chest where it shimmered and glowed figures and symbols creeping like frost across its surface in heart-of-gold.

"I asked you a question, lad. Where did you come by that staff?" The admiral was more insistent this time and banged his own taproot walking stick forcefully on the boards beneath their feet for emphasis; his eyes were a frozen color.

"It-it-it was my grandfather's!" Timmon managed. "He sent it with me when I left home."

"Not old Miter Strongtail?" The admiral was suspicious and took a slow sip from his tankard, lowering his head so that his hat once again eclipsed his eyes and his emotions.

"The same, sir." Timmon puffed his chest out as best he could and tried to inflate and look slightly tougher.

"Aye, Adm'ral. This lad came to us a few minutes ago, along with ol' Hoory Softflight here, sayin' he wants to sail the skies again." Brattleby Plateback stepped up behind Timmon, laid an oven-mitted claw over one shoulder and attempted to provide a little support.

Hoory also stepped forward, hooting softly, "'Tis good to see you again my good Admiral Featherscarf. It has surely been too long."

The admiral ruffled his feathers some, hackling his neck feathers so much that they nearly engulfed his head fully, "Aye, Hoory. 'Tis good to see your ol' self again too. And Brattleby you vouch for this lad, do you?"

"I do, Adm'ral."

"Might I inquire as to why he is covered in soup?"

Timmon fairly shivered with embarrassment, shifting his weight from one foot to the other and looking around somewhat nervously unsure what to say.

"Er, that would be m' fault, Adm'ral," Brattleby mumbled, picking a piece of still-lodged potato out of Timmon's shoulder fur. "Tossed last nigh's soup without lookin'."

"I see. And you wish to fly, lad? What was your name again, little thing?" Wattle Featherscarf leaned in a little closer, his ice-blue eyes just peeking out from under his hat and over his robustly large hooked beak, voice rattling like gravel.

"Timmon, sir. Timmon Strongtail, grandson of Miter Strongtail. From the Streams of the Valleys. I've come to find a ship and sail the skies." Timmon proudly turned his head a little so that his eagle feather fell into full view over his shoulder and from behind his neck.

"Ah, I see. An' the White-Eyed Wolf don't worry you none, eh? I'd say you're a fool. But you're young enough yet that it's probably still a touch of naivety. As for a ship, we got us a right old ship here. The Summerswill was my maiden vessel and the flagship of the Greenfleet for as many years as I care to say I ever sailed the skies. Not that I remember how many years that was, though, lad." Admiral Wattle Featherscarf winked then, and it was the first nonthreatening or nonfrightening gesture Timmon had seen from him. "Though, truth in full disclosure, lad, I'm old, too old to remember how old I am. And I'm afraid I don't remember the way through the ship's lock. Haven't for years, no sense in sailing an unsafe sky, so I fear I let myself forget. Heh, heh, heh!"

"The ship's lock?" Timmon was quite confused, "You lost the key?"

The entirety of the Summerswill Inn erupted into laughter, many creatures slamming their tankards and glasses onto their respective tables in fits of glee; there was an audible clatter of spoons, forks, and plates, and the goose at the bar honked so loudly that it nearly deafened Tim.

When the laughing has somewhat subsided, Admiral Wattle Featherscarf leaned closer to Timmon, his naked neck stretching to its full length, and his eyes staring directly into Timmon's as if through him.

"The ship's lock, lad, is far more than a simple key. It is the key."

"Show him, Admiral. I dare say he might not understand. And it is a visually stunning thing at that," Hoory exclaimed, stretching his wings to exemplify the enormity of the lock of which they were speaking.

"Very well then, follow me." Admiral Wattle Featherscarf leaned heavily on his taproot walking stick and set down his tankard. His coat, which had simply been sitting on his shoulders, slid off and onto the floor. "Grab my coat for me like a good creature, Brattleby, if you please."

"Yes, Admiral." Brattleby bent, a strange thing to watch a tortoise clad all in shell to do, and retrieved the admiral's coat.

Timmon followed the admiral to a door in the corner of the inn, a great oak square banded in iron that Brattleby also opened, heaving it with great strength. Behind they followed a tight hallway a long ways. The hallway grew dimmer and dimmer as they went, lit more and more sparingly with small candle lamps. At the end they came upon a similarly great door, and when Brattleby heaved open that door too, Timmon's breath caught in his throat.

Beyond the threshold of the door lay a small room in depth, though quite wide. The far wall was dominated by a series of concentric rings, all carved out of silverstone. The whole wheel was taller even than Brattleby and had an air of eminence and weight to it that made Tim think that it certainly must be as old as the foundations of the world itself. The stone rings, three in all with a central circle, were dominated by carved stone symbols of every different creature and element and natural thing. The whole wheel shimmered in the dim light of the room brilliantly like a sky full of blazing stars, and none noticed except Timmon that his staff was glowing an equally bright gold, thrumming with energy and vibrating so quickly that Timmon nearly dropped it to the floor when it first began; it startled him so. In awe Timmon's eyes locked on the central ring of the ship's lock, a small circle, much larger even than his whole head, though compared to the other three rings it seemed a small thing. On this center circle was carved a very deep paw-print; this, besides the rest of the lock, glowed the brightest gold that Timmon had ever gazed upon, and he was forced to avert his eyes as it rivaled the very sun in the sky.

"This, lad," the admiral gravelly voiced, waving a wing across the entire wheel before them, "is the ship's lock."

"I don't understand." Timmon cocked his head, as if that would aid his understanding.

"Lad, this is the ship's lock. It is carved from ancient silverstone, the likes of which cannot be found anywhere in the known world anymore." Admiral Wattle Featherscarf gestured with his taproot walking stick for emphasis, his misshapen hat sagging and lolling as he turned his head back and forth with his story. "The first and only vein of silverstone was discovered long ago before the measure of time known to us creatures of the Valleys. From it, the finest masons and smiths in the world created these wheels. Riddles woven into them by seers. Each airship, whether good or evil, bears a ship's lock just like the one before you; and each is bound by a secret code, deciphered only when the riddle of ship has been solved." The admiral tapped his walking stick on the floor with an audible thud, driving home the finality of this statement.

"Then what is the riddle?" Timmon asked eagerly.

"I don't remember, lad. I simply don't. I've grown very old since the last time the Summerswill set sail, and in the years that have passed my mind has become clouded and dark, where once it was calculating and lucid."

"Does anyone?"

"Doubtful, lad. I fear a good many creatures like us who once proudly sailed the skies have become beasts that are cursed to wander the lands by means of our own feet or fly only as high as our wings allow. Which, compared to the flight of an airship, is little more than standing at the base of a great mountain, when one used to stand at its apex," Hoory added, clicking his beak apprehensively.

Timmon felt he needed to sit; he was so distraught. To have come so far, only to find that his one dream—his single goal, this airship—was grounded, and not a single creature knew the answer to the riddle to make her fly, let alone the riddle itself. A jingling of bells behind him, something like the shuffling of papers, made Timmon turn his head to see who approached.

From down the hallways came the pair of squirrels who had been serving the other creatures at the inn. One was clearly the elder, though both had manes of braided hair, and bells and bangles woven into their bushy curving tails, and both wore painted vests of a hundred brilliant colors. Behind them awkwardly waddled the goose who had been seated at the bar, a veritable ream of papers stuffed into his belt, the loupe that had graced his eye now hung on a chain about his very, very long neck, and his tricornered hat was about to falloff of the top of his head, and did when he let out a loud honk. The nearest squirrel, the younger, bent to pick it up and place it back on his head, softly saying, "Oh, Isaac."

Brattleby waved a claw and introduced the three new creatures as such, “Timmon, may I present, the Lady Teera Proudleap, once deckmaster of the airship Summerswill. Her daughter and a beautiful young maid to boot, the Lady Neesa!” The last he added with a note of chagrin, quite like annoyance, “And the goose who sits at the bar and pores over maps, this is Isaac Southwinter.”

“Honk!”

“A pleasure. Timmon was it?” The eldest squirrel shook his paw with a grip far firmer than Timmon would have imagined.

“Pff.” The younger squirrel was not quite as pleased to meet Timmon, he assuaged. Instead Timmon bent one knee and touched his forehead with one paw, a gesture as polite and respectful as he could muster. Rather than accept the gesture, or as Timmon had dared hope, blush at his chivalrous manner, or what Timmon had hoped was a chivalrous manner, she merely puffed up her cheeks and turned on her heel, walking back down the hallway.

“My apologies, Timmon. She is of that age.”

“It isn’t a problem, Lady Proudleap.”

“Teera, please, lad. And this is Isaac. He isn’t much in the way of lengthy introductions or an evening of conversation, but truth be told, from a squirrel who has sailed the skies and been to the ends of this world, he does have quite a way with maps.”

“Isaac, a pleasure.” Timmon held out his paw, received with a bundle of Isaac Southwinter’s wing feathers.

“Good ’ter meet ’ya, lad, honk!”

“Would that I could use your cartography skills, sadly, it appears as if my journey ends here.” Isaac hung his head, clearly distressed.

Timmon was suddenly distracted by the thrum of his own blackwood staff in his paw, for now, as it had faded before; the staff had just again burst into a shining miasma of light, bright gold and shredding rays of pure brilliance through the room that housed the ship’s lock. In that moment, Timmon thought he saw, but could not be sure for a moment, the perfect pristine visage of his grandfather, staring back at him from the shaft of Timmon’s blackwood staff, speaking, though no sound emanated.

It was then that Timmon remembered . . .

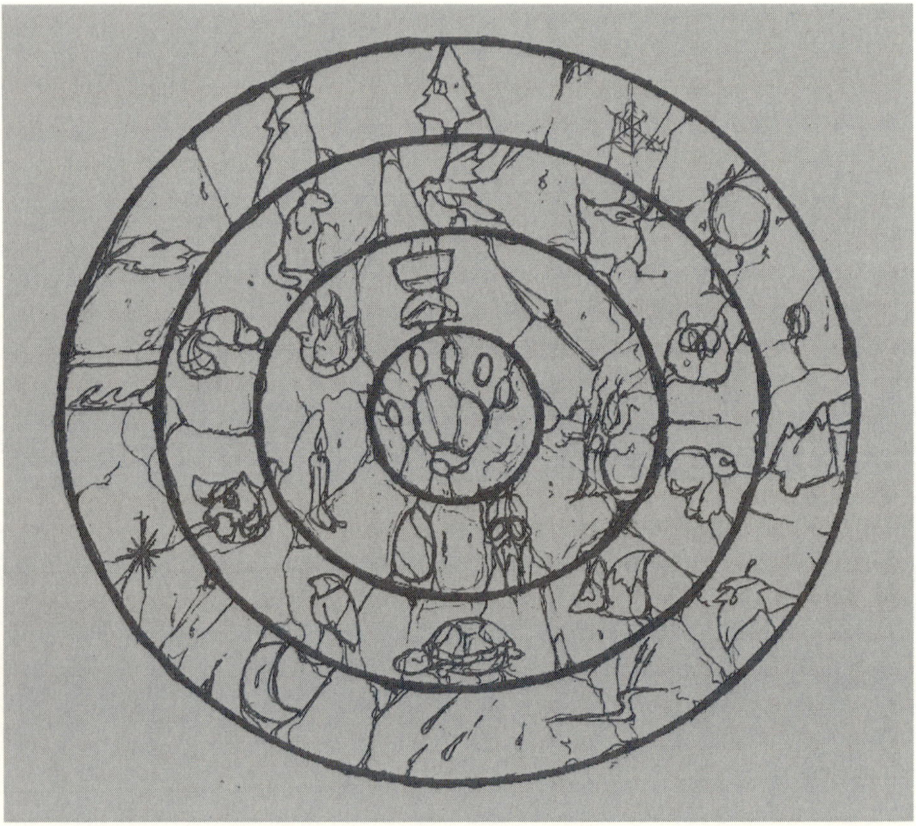

He thought back to the night, not so long ago, though it seemed as if ages had passed, that he had left his family's longboat and called upon his grandfather one last time to say goodbye. He thought and thought, scrunching his eyes up in deep frustration, trying desperately to remember the first line.

"What beast that embraces two parts of the world?" Timmon managed to utter under his breath, still thinking deeply. He did not notice the deafening silence that suddenly cut through the ship's lock room. Nor did he notice when Admiral Wattle Featherscarf stretched out his long pink wrinkled neck and brought his great beak within a hairs breadth of Timmon's nose and asked,

"What in all the Valleys did you just say, lad?"

"What beast—," Timmon began, but the admiral cut him off.

"I know what you said, whelp! It was a rhetorical question. Where did you hear that?" His ice-blue eyes were shimmering with intent.

"My grandfather told me a verse the night I left home. He never said what it meant. He was still asleep I think."

"He knew the riddle then. He wasn't supposed to-the ship's riddle is only known to the captain himself and passed from one captain to another upon transfer of the leadership of a vessel. Yet you tell me you know the riddle?"

"I-I-I suppose. I tried to memorize it, but it was quite long, sir. And it was very strange."

"It's a riddle, lad. They seldom make sense without the answer." The admiral was beginning to speak very shortly with Timmon, clearly perplexed with the idea that someone aside from the ship's captain had known the riddle that opened the ship's lock; though, unbeknownst to Timmon, he was also the slightest bit relieved, like the final dying coal in a fire, that relief smoldered and was brighter than his frustration though he did not show it. The admiral was going to fly again, that he knew. "Do you remember the rest?"

"Something about snakes and sunlight. Does it mean the Summerswill? Sun and summer and light?"

"To protect the ship's integrity the riddle associated with the ship's lock often had little to do with the name of the ship." Hoory clicked his beak, "Sorry, good Admiral. I wanted to throw out a little fact that I knew." He hooted and settled back away from the admiral whose feathers had hackled themselves, and he looked quite the vulture at this point.

"Indeed."

"I'm sorry, I just don't remember the rest." Timmon hung his head.

"Honk!"

Brattleby put an oven-mitted claw on Timmon's shoulder reassuringly and said, "Tim, try looking at the wheel, maybe it'll jog your memory?"

So Timmon craned his head, curled his tail around his feet, and stared for a long time at the ship's lock before him. The silverstone rings carved with many symbols, all of which he thought on long and hard, trying desperately to remember the lines his grandfather had uttered in his half-sleep.

All the creatures about him kept silent, and as minutes turned to hours, they gradually began to take their leave, seeking food and drink back in the dining room of the Inn of the Rising Sun, the Summerswill. Each gave Timmon a reassuring pat or a solemn look as they walked past. Hoory left him a small handful of the nuts that they had roasted the other night, and Teera Proudleap brought him a mug of steaming water with a slice of lemon in it to warm his thoughts and his body.

Nibbling on roasted nuts and gingerly sipping his steaming lemon water, Timmon found himself sitting before the great ship's lock, his tail curled about his crossed legs, his blackwood staff resting before him. He barely noticed the dying of the candles that lit the room, who slowly lost the remainder of their wax while he sat, and a good many of them guttered with no wick left to fuel them as Timmon sat and pondered and wondered.

Timmon's mind was a miasma of thoughts. He could not concentrate on one idea before another had replaced it, and he found it harder than ever to focus. The subtle glow of the silverstone ship's lock was all the light that remained in the small room, and there were no windows to the outside; as such, Timmon had no idea how much time had passed, and whether or not it was night or day. His lemon water was long gone, and his roasted nuts were little more than hulls, much like the ship's hull in which he sat.

What beast that embraces two halves of this entire world.

He thought long and hard, looking predominantly at the second ring of the wheel, for it was all carvings of beasts and birds and other creatures, one or two of which were so worn and ancient that he had trouble discerning what they could be. One or the other might have been a fox or a raccoon, although having never seen either of these creatures he was unsure.

Is nestled 'twixt hard tail and wing unfurled?

There was an otter, like himself to be sure. It was nestled betwixt an eagle with spread wings and a hunched over carving of a beaver. He thought that perhaps this symbol was the answer to the first part of the riddle, as otters spend just as much time in the water as on land, if not more. Timmon thought that perhaps that's what the two halves of the world were, soil and water. Though there was also a turtle in the second ring, a creature that spends just as much time on land and in the water, and this to was beside the carving of a songbird, though the songbird's wings were tucked down, not spread like the eagles. Beside the turtle was a figure Timmon could not completely make out, though he surmised it was a fox because of its large tail, capped in color, as if dipped into paint, though the silverstone gave no hint of what that color may be.

Timmon was almost sure of the first part of the riddle, after many hours of thinking, though it hardly made any sense that the first line of the riddle pertained to the second ring of the ship's lock. He wished the admiral were with him to answer his questions. But the admiral did not remember the solution or even the riddle itself, and Timmon had made up his mind to not leave the room of the ship's lock until he had solved the riddle, and the Summerswill could once again be airborne, with Timmon Strongtail at its helm.

Whence the sun has cracked her rays to splinters, opposite snakes whose scales harden in winters.

This line Timmon could not make any sense of. The outer ring was all natural symbols, but there were thirteen in all, so nothing was truly opposite another, but rather was opposite two symbols, as near as Timmon could guess. The sun itself was an orb ringed by tiny triangular rays of light and was appropriately opposite a star and a crescent moon. Timmon thought that the star might be referred to in the riddle by splinters of light, but he could not be sure. He was certain that the pine tree and mountains and leaf and spider web probably didn't have anything to do with the riddle, so he all but forgot about those symbols. Then again, Timmon thought, spider webs covered in morning dew had a way of breaking the sun's light in an awfully pretty way. And he was sure that one symbol on the outer ring of the ship's lock was meant to be a crudely carved representation of lightning, which was not quite rays of light, although it certainly resembled splinters. Despite the star and the lightning and the spider web all being possible clues to splintered light, Timmon could not for anything think of what a snake whose scales freeze in winter might be, besides a snake. Everything froze in hard winters, and Timmon saw no reason why a snake's scales wouldn't freeze in winter, although there was no representation of a snake on the ship's lock, and for that portion of the clue, Timmon was hopelessly lost.

O'er the consumption of all is her birth, to all new things of all new worth.

For the final clue, Timmon was unsure of which ring the riddle was referring because as far as he could tell, the riddle itself was out of order or the rings were out of order, he couldn't tell.

Hoory had said that the riddles of airship's lock often had little to do with the ship's title at all as it made the riddles harder to solve, so Timmon saw no reason why the riddle would be in order at all with respect to the rings on the ship's lock.

Timmon buried his head in frustration in his paws willing himself not to cry but sobbing a little all the same. It seemed hopeless, trying to figure out this riddle. Despite it all, Timmon sat stoically with his legs crossed, and his tail curled around himself, staring at the softly glowing silverstone of the ship's lock, thinking as hard as he could until his head began to hurt.

He would solve this riddle if it meant sitting alone in the dark, and Timmon told himself he would not leave until the riddle was solved.

By the next morning, Neesa Proudleap found Timmon sound asleep, his head and neck curled into his breast, still sitting cross-legged with his tail wrapped around his body, his blackwood staff glowing palely and resting against his shoulder.

She had brought with her a small tray of food. Buttered biscuits, roasted walnuts stuffed with mushrooms, and a mound of grilled onions topped the tray; and she bore a tankard of steaming lemon water in her other paw. These she set down beside Timmon and gently nudged his shoulder; the bells in her tail jingling slightly as she did so.

"Nuh," Timmon shuddered slightly, barely awake.

"My mother asked me to bring you something to eat, you've been here all night, you know?"

"Mmmzzim. Wha'?" Timmon lifted his head up, eyes slits of slumber, and looked around until he found the source of the voice that had woken him. "Thnk's."

"You're welcome. Why are you here, otter?" Neesa folded her arms over her breast.

Timmon, now slightly more awake managed to answer, "I want to fly."

"We all want to fly. The thing is, none of us are ever going to be able to. I'm not sure if you've noticed, otter, but the eagles are gone," she harrumphed.

Timmon stood, helping himself up with his blackwood staff, bent and took a buttered biscuit from the tray, for he was actually quite hungry and said through bits of biscuit, "I know the eagles have left, everyone does. But that isn't a reason not to try. The world, as I've been told, is a vast and wonderful place, and I mean to see all of it."

"Starting with this little room and this large lock, you mean?"

"If I must pass through this to see what my grandfather wanted me to, then I will."

"Yes, your grandfather." Neesa cocked her head, as if thinking, "My mother says that he sailed with her, long ago. She spoke quite highly of him and said that he was the best buccaneer she ever knew."

"I only know what he told me in stories, and as fantastic as they were, I only ever thought they were just that, stories. Now that I know that it was all true, that the world really is an amazing place, I mean to make the most of the life that I have." Timmon's eyes teared up a little at the thought of his grandfather back home and how far away that was now.

"You miss him?" Neesa said nothing of Tim's tears but simply stared at the ship's lock, glimmering slightly before them.

"I do," Timmon said, turning to Neesa a little, catching her eye. "Would you like to come with me?"

"Well, someone has to, if you ever figure out this riddle. Actually my mother asked me to come speak with you. She heard from that old owl, Hoory was it?"

"Hoory, yes."

"She heard that you might need some help with that staff of yours. Fighting with it, I mean."

"I suppose I do," Timmon held the staff in his paws affectionately.

"Come outside then, take a break from all of this riddling, and I'll show you what I know. It'll clear your head."

"All right." Timmon took another buttered biscuit with him as he stood and munched on it thoughtfully as they walked out the corridor and through the sleepy morning light of the Inn of the Rising Sun, out into the brisk air and clear skies of dawn.

Timmon was not prepared for what happened next . . .

The swift crack of a branch across Timmon's face knocked him to the dirt, flat on his bottom. Not a moment later a second blow struck the ground just to Timmon's left.

"Weapon up!" Neesa shouted, bringing her branch back behind her head for a third blow. Timmon managed to lift his blackwood staff above his head with one paw, parrying the strike, which struck the shaft of dark wood and heart-of-gold, rattling Timmon's arm to the bone.

"What are you doing?" Timmon asked loudly, rolling across his back and into a crouch, his blackwood staff held firmly in both paws, still wondering where Neesa had grabbed a branch from so quickly.

"Teaching you! The White-Eyed Wolf won't hesitate when he swings for your head!" She cut a wide swath with her branch, a cut that was aimed low toward Timmon's belly, a cut that Timmon countered with his staff clumsily but was too slow to stop the blow that followed immediately after and caught him across the jaw, knocking him again to the dirt.

Neesa danced on the balls of her feet in a light circle around Timmon, the bells in her tail jingling merrily, twirling the branch in her hand as if it were a cutlass. Timmon managed to find his way to his feet, holding his cheek with one paw as it had already began to swell.

"That really hurt, Neesa."

"It'll hurt a lot more when the weapon is made of sharpened iron!" She lashed out again with her branch, a blow that Timmon again caught with his blackwood staff before she danced back into a fencing posture, spinning the branch with one paw.

"Where did you learn all of this?"

"My mother," she struck out with the branch, snapping it on Timmon's unguarded shoulder. "She taught me to use a weapon to protect myself. Something you clearly need to learn, the pirates would make mince out of you." Twice more she struck out, quick as a flash, the first blow caught Timmon in the thigh, the second cracked down on his tail painfully.

Timmon barely noticed the glowing of the blackwood staff in his hands nor the humming vibrations that ran through it then or the pendulous way that it began to rotate in his paw, moving as if by itself, the pictures and stories etched into its surface reflecting the ideas of a thousand battles long forgotten as it led Timmon on the offensive. The first blow he laid out was a high smashing attack from behind his head, followed quickly by a strike at Neesa's knee, and a third blow to her opposite side just at her midsection. All three blows struck in quick succession, and she only managed to block the first, the second and third caught her off guard they came so quickly. The surprise in her eyes was almost written in stone, and she retaliated with a flurry of her own attacks, each of which Timmon deftly blocked, the ringing cracks of wood on wood resounding in the yard outside the Inn of the Rising Sun.

"How—did—you—do—that?" She gasped between blows.

"I—don't know!" Timmon chocked back as he blocked each blow, the blackwood staff in his paws moving as if with its own mind, remembering how it had served its bearers in so many battles before.

They traded blows for what seemed like hours, and the constant ring of branch on blackwood echoed through the morning. When both were tired and near gasping for breath they found themselves facing each other, each gripping their respective weapons firmly, braced for another attack before a call rang out from within the Inn.

"Brekkist!"

"That'll be Brattleby. I suppose this morning training session is ended." Neesa set her branch down beside the entrance to the inn and turned asking, "That staff is something special isn't it? My mother told me it would be, but I had to see it for myself."

"It is as special as any gift."

"Yes, but that gift may one day save your life. He was a wise creature, your grandfather, giving it to you."

"He is wise." Timmon held his blackwood staff closely, the shaft was still swirling with golden smoke and figures and scenes flitted across its surface, "Shall we get something to eat?"

"Of course. I want to do this again, after breakfast. If you're going to be our captain, then you must need to learn to fight. And even with your fine staff to teach you, you've got a lot of learning to do."

"Captain?"

"Wait!" Timmon called, "Captain? Me?"

"Yes, of course you. Whole else?" Neesa called back over her shoulder as they strode together into the dining room of the Inn of the Rising Sun where dishes already clattered and a number of creatures had begun to eat their morning meal.

"I mean . . . I guess. Okay, I can be captain . . . I guess." Timmon picked a chair opposite from where Neesa had just settled down at a small round table of old wood near the far corner of the room. It was only moments before Brattleby appeared beside them, bearing two heaping plates of fried mushrooms, green beans, and sliced tomato topped with garlic, two hunks of fire-seared hard bread, sopping wet with butter, and a pair of tankards filled with chilled berry juice.

"Ere's yer brekkist my two youn' warriors. Eat up!" Brattleby lumbered away after setting down their plates before them to serve other creatures, his massive oven-mitted claws swaying like pendulums at his sides.

"You're going to have to do better than 'I guess,' Timmon. Your crew is expecting you to lead them to the skies against the Wolf, into adventure."

"M-m-my crew?" Timmon was quite dumbstruck at this point.

"Yes, Tim. Don't you get it? You came here looking for adventure, looking for the life of a buccaneer. Now the world is giving you that very opportunity. You might as well seize it because if you continue to dilly-dally it may go up in smoke."

She continued, "We all met last evening, a lot of us. While you were staring at the ship's lock trying to decipher that old riddle."

"So you know the answer!?" Timmon's eyes lit up.

"No. No! We don't. If we did we'd have been in the air long ago. But the creatures here believe you can solve it, and if that's true, then we're behind you completely. To tell you the truth, most of the old-timers here have just been waiting for someone to come along and solve the riddle, anyone really. Then you came along with Miter's blackwood staff, and well, they thought that their salvation had walked through that front door covered in soup."

"Who exactly is behind me?"

"Isaac and I. Brattleby, my mother, Hoory, even old Admiral Featherscarf is willing to fly one more time." Neesa took a long drink from her tankard of berry juice, wiping her mouth with the back of her paw, "So what'll it be otter?"

"I've got a riddle to figure out." Timmon was up like a shot, shouldering his blackwood staff and as an afterthought, grabbing his plate of breakfast, bounding for the back door that led to the ship's lock, throwing it open and disappearing down the hallway.

What beast that embraces two halves of this entire world, is nestled 'twixt hard tail and wing unfurled? Whence the sun hast cracked her rays to splinters, opposite snakes whose scales harden in winters. O'er the consumption of all is her birth, to all new things of all new worth.

The otter, Timmon was sure of. A creature that treads both water and over land, its figure was carved between that of a beaver and an eagle with outstretched wings.

Snakes with hardened winter scales was finally making sense. Timmon had thought that the riddle had meant a literal snake, though now he could see that the outer ring was all symbols of nature and her elements, and snake was meant in more descriptive terms. Across from a jagged lightning bolt, clearly meant by splintered rays of sun, was a winding stream curtained by cattails. In winter the surface of streams often iced over especially if they were smaller snaking streams. The second line of the riddle now made sense. It also seemed to fit true that an otter and a stream were connected, and so the symbol on the outer ring must certainly be a stream.

The final line still irked Timmon. The inner ring was made up of seven symbols. An hourglass, a leafless tree, a candle, flames, a spear, what looked like an egg, and a morbidly carved skull that fairly dripped and oozed rot, though it was carved from silverstone. When Timmon thought of consumption, he thought of eating or engulfing something that it seemed unlikely a tree or a spear or an hourglass would do. Birth brought to mind the symbol of the egg, though he thought of creatures who were born from eggs as hatching and not necessarily being born. Timmon was left with the idea that fire consumed all in its path, and his grandfather had once told him how forest fires are a part of life, and that when a forest is cleansed in flame, it often grows anew, lusher, and more brilliant than before. So skeptically, Timmon thought that the third line of the riddle referred to the etched symbol of flames.

An otter, a stream, and flames.

Summerswill.

Timmon thought perhaps he was missing something, but rather than sit idly by and wonder, Timmon dug his feet into the floorboards and braced himself with his tail. He grabbed hold of the deepest notches he could find in the silverstone rings with his paws, one paw gripping the crescent of the moon, another wedged deep into the fat body of a falling raindrop and heaved the outer ring around until the cattailed stream was oriented perfectly at the top of the ship's lock.

Next he firmly gripped the shell of the carved turtle with both paws and ground the otter figure into place beneath the stream. Sweat had begun to form in droplets across his forehead and chin and shoulders. The silverstone ship's lock was a stubborn old thing as ancient and mysterious as it was stiff with disuse.

Finally, Timmon grabbed hold of one of the eye sockets of the gaunt skull and of the egg's shell and gritted his teeth as he struggled to force the final symbol, the flames into place beneath the otter and the stream. With one great heaving lurch of muscle, Timmon sank the flames into place and stood back, listening intently to what sounded like a thousand, thousand great metal and stone and wooden locks turning and tumbling behind the wall of silverstone. The sounds of creaks and clinks and clacks echoed through the hull of the ship, and a great light like that of the moon in its full splendor began to shiver and ripple through the carved paw print in the center of the ship's lock. Needlepoints of light became honed blades of fiery white evanescence streaking out from the etched lines of the paw print. Timmon Strongtail had to shield his eyes from the brightness of it all and was quite unaware of the rattling and dancing of his own blackwood staff in the corner of the room.

Arm outstretched, Timmon placed his paw over its near-mirror replica; the silverstone was warm at the touch and light arced out from beneath his fur, and with a final grating of stone, the central circle of the ship's lock sunk in like a pressed button and all around Timmon, the world lurched.

Unseen cogs and wheels and mechanisms fairly screamed back to life. The engine deep within the bowels of the Summerswill, beneath and beyond the ship's lock roared in response, and Timmon felt the floor beneath him shift and give way.

Far down the corridor, beyond the door at Tim's back, creatures of all kinds howled, yelped and squawked. The most prominent was the nefarious and incessant honking of Isaac Southwinter. Timmon looked to his feet where his blackwood staff lay aglow with a fantastic iridescent light. The images that swirled over its surface were of a thousand, thousand airships taking flight, launching themselves from wet and dry-dock alike, wings outstretched and sails billowing with wind. Tim's eyes shone with tears of happiness and ecstasy, and he leaped into the air, pumping one fist in triumph.

"I did it!"

Behind him the door burst open, and the light of the hallway flooded into the ship's lock chamber, silhouetted there in the shivering candlelight stood Admiral Wattle Featherscarf, Brattleby Plateback, and Hoory Softflight. The admiral was the first to shout,

"What have you done?"

"I solved it!" Timmon shouted, spinning around to meet the admiral.

"You did? I hadn't noticed." Hoory clicked his beak cheekily.

"We're aloft," Brattleby added, flipping a soup spoon in one claw to emphasize.

"We are?" Timmon asked, barely able to speak. He snatched up his brightly glowing blackwood staff and sprinted for the door, knocking Hoory to the floor in the process. Timmon shouldered down the hallway into the common room where he found a complete up-shod mess. The creatures who had occupied the tables in and around the common room of the Inn of the Rising Sun had fallen out of their chairs and up-ended all of their great wooden tables. Food and drink was spilled and slicked across every surface of the room. Timmon literally slid into the room an a crust of hard bread over a face of spilled tomato soup. He swung wildly with one paw and managed to catch the back of a bench; digging in his nails, he pulled himself up a little and looked around.

Teera and Neesa Proudleap both wore frowns as crescent as the moon midmonth and were covered in dripping beverage and food. A host of other creatures who had happened by the inn were piled haphazardly atop one another, equally drenched in foodstuffs and liquid. All of the glasses behind the bar had fallen from their shelves and clinked and clanked their way about the creatures' feet. The roaring fire in the hearth, thankfully, had not been terribly disturbed, and only a few embers burned beyond the heart stones, although the iron hooks and pots of soup that hung over the flames had been dislodged and swung this way and that, casting their contents over the entire room.

Finally, in the corner, covered completely by a pile of ragged parchment maps, sodden with stews and soups and steamed vegetables, was the twitchy, erratic form of Isaac Southwinter, loupe askew, tricornered hat completely gone.

"Honk! Honk! Honk! Honk! Honk! Honk! Honk! Honk! Honk! Honk!"

Timmon stared in a circle around at the creatures that surrounded him, feeling a little ashamed that his triumph had caused all of this ruckus. Then with a soft beat of heart from his blackwood staff, Timmon Strongtail whipped his eagle feather from before his eyes and said to all assembled beneath, before, and around him, even those who were upside down,

"Let's go look outside."

Neesa and Teera Proudleap were the first to stand and offer their hands to Timmon, who led them as cordially as he could to the door that had once been the entrance to the Inn of the Rising Sun. The other creatures followed, among them Brattleby, Hoory, Isaac, and Admiral Wattle Featherscarf.

Approaching the door, Timmon laid a paw on the handle, his blackwood staff clutched near his heart by the other. He turned to the assembled creatures behind him and said,

"I give you the sky." With that, Timmon threw open the door. Heads crowded the door, clasping for a look out into the blues and whites of the heights where only eagles soar. They bumbled over one another until each and every one, upon reaching the threshold of the door, shook their heads in disgust, rounded, and returned to the common room to pick up what was left of their meals. Timmon, chest heaving with exuberance, finally turned and looked himself out the door . . .

. . . and saw only grass and a cobblestone walkway, and a little ways below, a sign in the shape of a noonday disc that read, "The Inn of the Rising Sun."

Timmon thought that he might burst into tears of frustration then, and his jaw dropped to what felt like the floor. Beyond the threshold of the door lay only what had lain beyond the threshold of the door before when the ship had been grounded. In disbelief, Timmon stood in the doorway, one paw on either side of the frame and his head far below the lintel of the very large door. Timmon shut his eyes once, twice, and then three times, each time hoping to open them again to the true scene of brilliantly colored clouds flying past them at amazing speeds, to no avail. Then he was thrust forward, a force caught him in the center of his back, like a kick or the punch of a fist.

Timmon sprawled face forward into the cobble and dirt outside of the Inn of the Rising Sun. Spitting grit and shale from his teeth, Timmon turned his head over his shoulder and looked to see the form of Admiral Wattle Featherscarf in the doorway, his taproot walking stick outstretched.

"Why did you push me?" Timmon could not think of anything worse than adding insult to injury at that moment.

"Fell a little did'ja?" Wattle chuckled a little under his breath, his hackles shivering.

"Yeah. Because you pushed me."

"Little further than a'fore?"

"Huh?"

"Look, lad."

Timmon turned his head a little in the gravel and cobble and noticed something strange. A slight gap now existed between the earth and the Summerswill's hull. It was barely a fraction, a blade of grass, but it was there. Timmon's eyes lit up, and he clambered to his feet as quickly as he could, though this was quite clumsily. Shaking the dirt and debris from his fur and striking himself in the face twice to ensure that he was not dreaming, Timmon asked the admiral, "Are we aloft?"

"Captain, 'tis but a hair, but we are aloft. At your command!"

Some hours later, the admiral had managed to assemble all of the creatures who wished to stay and listen beneath the boughs of a mighty oak tree. They were a mismatched crew of every species and wore a patchwork quilt of different types of clothes that spanned every color imaginable. Atop a small moss-covered boulder beneath the tree, much like the one on which he had first discovered his blackwood staff's true power, stood Timmon. Staff in hand and his eagle feather blowing slightly in the breeze, Timmon tried to look more buccaneer-ish or regal than he truly felt. In truth, he was quite nervous, and his stomach turned in knots like the rolling of the seas with each breath he took, but he clutched his staff close and took an enormous amount of comfort from it.

Beside him, standing next to the boulder, bent with old age and with his hackles raising and lowering sporadically, leaned Admiral Wattle Featherscarf on his aged taproot walking stick. His great floppy hat was a slithering miasma of cloth and patches and hid his eyes from sight more often than not, and Timmon for the life of him could not figure out how the old vulture could see well enough to address the small gathering before them; but then again, being an admiral, Timmon supposed he was used to addressing crews.

"Al'righ you lot. This here is Timmon Strongtail, the grandson of ol' Miter Strongtail. Some o' you may remember him from your ol' skyfarin' days. He was a grand ol' otter, and as fine a warrior as any I have ever met. None of you will doubt that, n' if you d you can turn tail and walk t'other way." The admiral arced his great leathery neck back and forth, looking each potential crew member in the eye as he did so, staring straight through them. When none of the assembled creatures left, he continued,

"This lad here, he solved the riddle o' the ship's lock, in a night nonetheless, which is a lot more than I'll say for any o' you. He's got the gift or some such. Like as not he can see things in that staff that none o' us others can. An' seein' as he's the one who made that there hulk"—he waved his taproot walking stick in the direction of the lazily floating airship Summerswill that idled in its original position, albeit a few inches higher—"move an' come back to life. Well, tradition dictates that the captain be the only creature who knows the riddle an' its subsequent answer. We all agreed on that point?" Featherscarf looked around, hat flopping back and forth as he did so at every assembled creature.

Before Timmon, all of their heads bobbed up and down. There must be thirty creatures here and they want me to be their captain. Oh, grandfather, if you could only see me now! Timmon thought.

"Al'righ then. You! There! Hare! What's your name, n' how can you serve Cap'n Strongtail?" Featherscarf thrust his knotted taproot walking stick in the direction of a ragged-looking young brown hare wearing an unraveling hat that his ears poked awkwardly through and an old gray jacket.

"M-m-m-me, sir?"

"Yes, rabbit. You."

"I'm Norrey Diggaburrow. I'm really good wif' ropes n' things."

"Can you tie a butterfly knot, Diggaburrow?" Featherscarf produced a length of rope from somewhere unseen within his old sailing jacket and heaved it at the quite frightened hare.

"Y-y-y-yes, I can!" Norrey Diggaburrow's paws moved swiftly, flitting over one another and through and over and over the rope, faster and faster until he held out what looked like a smashed acorn made of hempen rope.

"Excellent! Welcome to the crew of the Summerswill!" Admiral Featherscarf cracked his taproot staff hard on the boulder on which Timmon stood to emphasize. In turn, Timmon leaned low and spoke in a whisper to the admiral.

"Are you sure that was the correct knot?"

"Lad, you have a lot o' learnin' to do. That was a fine butterfly knot, n' the hare can learn quick, we could use him tendin' the sails and the tie offs."

"Tie offs?"

"Lad, let this ol' admiral pick you your crew, while you sit pretty up there on your rock. I'm the skyfarer, n' your the grandson o' my greatest ol' friend. Proven twice over. If there's one last adventure out there, we're takin' it."

"Thank you." Timmon looked down at the admiral, not from high as they were near eye-to-eye with Timmon's lean, and said softly,

"No need ta' thank me, Captain. Let's just take the skies."

"Agreed."

With that, the admiral swirled outward from Timmon; his feathers and hat and coat all awhirl around him as he did so, taproot walking stick raised high and he fairly shouted,

"Who else has somethin' to offer the captain of the great airship Summerswill?"

"Honk!"

"Southwinter, righ' this way!"

By the time the sun was beginning to set behind the Summerswill, its rays slipping through the fallow sails of the ship, turning their worn white to a hundred brilliant shades of orange and yellow and pink and deep purple, Admiral Wattle Featherscarf had assembled a ragtag crew of creatures of all sizes. Included among the wayward band were Hoory Softflight, now the medical officer for the ship, given his talents with herbal remedies and poultices. Neesa Proudleap was named weapons officer. Norrey Diggaburrow was named master of sails and fidgeted frightfully, as if uncomfortable with the idea of holding such a responsibility. Brattleby Plateback had assumed his current position of head chef of the Inn of the Rising Sun in a more official capacity as ship's cook. Admiral Wattle Featherscarf had named himself first mate, both at his own behest and at Timmon Strongtail's request because Tim knew he would need the wisdom of the old skyfaring bird if he were to manage an airship properly, or at all. Finally, Isaac Southwinter, the ubiquitous goose, had been named navigator. He had been so elated at the appointment that he honked for several minutes straight before he managed a humble "Thank you."

The remainder of the crew was made up of creatures Timmon had not yet met or only knew by sight. They were a menagerie of squirrels, mice, chipmunks, sparrows, hares, a single matronly badger, and a young-looking fox who seemed to think he was quite out of place.

Without guidance, Timmon was quite alone in what to do. Once the old Admiral Featherscarf had selected his medical officer, weapons officer, himself as first mate, deckhands, chef, sail master, Tim was at a loss for what to do next.

In the dying shadow of the day, Timmon managed to take a moment from the admiral. All the other creatures, now crew members, were dining at great feasting tables that had been dragged outside of the former Inn of the Rising Sun by those involved and the many creatures who had remained present for the festivities or were actual members of the crew of the newly airborne Summerswill were busy regaling each other with stories or celebrating the soon-to-be launch of the first airship since the White-Eyed Wolf took the skies.

Once Timmon had managed to escort the admiral from the party for a moment, he broached a subject he had been reluctant to address for some time.

"Admiral, this is really happening isn't it?" Timmon was backlit by the failing light of the sun, barely silhouetting the Summerswill and her flaccid sails, the purple and blues of night framing the shifting gold and black of Timmon's blackwood staff like a curtain.

"Lad, you solved a riddle that no one has known for years. You took this fight into your hands and fought it, what little part of it you could manage for the time being.

And. You. Won. The first airship in the longest time is aloft, and being nothing else, this would still stick in the White-Eyed Wolf's craw. Creatures like us were meant to fare the skies, and you've perhaps brought that back."

"But, Captain? I can't do that!" Timmon was filled with more doubt than he had believed could fill him, and he was at the least distraught.

"You can, and I'll guide you, lad. See, the thing is, it's tradition, you being the one who solved and remembered the riddle to the ship's lock and all, but maybe you do deserve this? Maybe so? But who's to say. Let it rest for tonight lad for we take off in the morning."

"Unfurl the sails, Mr. Diggaburrow! Lock open n' functioning, Captain Strongtail! All crew members tied in n' secure?"

"Aye!"

"Aye!"

"Aye! Aye! Aye!"

Admiral wattle Featherscarf cocked his great floppy hat back on his head and struck his taproot walking stick out straight, standing as tall as could muster at the prow of the airship Summerswill. "Up n' away then, lads n' lasses!"

Belowdecks, Timmon Strongtail could hear the cries from the admiral and stood before the massive silverstone ship's lock. Standing his blackwood staff against the deep red wood of the ship's wall, he took the outer ring of the ship's lock in his paws, gripping it firmly as he had before by the crescent moon and starburst, pushing his weight down and forward and tugging with all of his might until the outer ring was in position, as it seemed to have shifted during the night, out of position. The middle ring he held firmly by the owl's ear tufts and again put all of his weight behind his shove, pressing off with his tail as well as he could. Finally he took the central ring by the guttering candle, holding the carving as he might a staff; it was etched so deeply. Muscles in his shoulders and stomach flexing taut, he forced the final ring, and the flames, into position. Stream, Otter, and Flames properly aligned, he for the second time in his life, depressed the central button of the ship's lock.

The button depressed a little easier this time, and the light that burst forth was like a beacon. Silver-blue veins of light spread like creeper vines through the silverstone ship's lock, and Timmon's blackwood staff hummed with golden spiraling light in sync with the light of the lock like two hearts throbbing in unison.

Taking his blackwood staff from its resting place, energy humming out of it like a living thing, Timmon turned to leave the room, calling out as he did, "Lock engaged!"

The admiral's call back was muffled by the audible throb of the ship's lock and its passage through the deck above, but Timmon heard it quite clearly, "Take the helm then, Captain!"

Timmon strode up on deck to something he was quite unaccustomed to seeing. The entirety of the crew of the Summerswill was assembled, those with weapons had them drawn across their hearts, those without had their fists clenched over their breasts in salute. Each and everyone was strapped about the waist by a leather leash or a length of hempen rope so that none would fall if they encountered choppy skies, and all had a look in their eyes that Timmon could not put words to, but said simply, adventure.

Tears forming in his eyes and love in his heart, Timmon could barely manage for several moments to find something to say. Finally, unable to hide his face, as that seemed a very uncaptainlike thing to do, he blinked back his tears and managed, "I thank you, all of you. This will be, I hope, the greatest time for any of us. We go together not as a captain and crew but as friends. Anyone who knows, is there any paint on this ship?"

The look on every member of Timmon's crew was quite the same, befuddlement.

"Uh, paint captain?" It was Neesa Proudleap who spoke, lowering her rapier just a hair, clearly puzzled.

Brattleby spoke next, his voice more of a gruff utterance than anything, "Look 'ere, folks, the cap'n wants paint, find 'im some bleedin' paint!" This was accompanied by another several moments of stunned silence before all the creatures of the crew scurried, hopped, and lumbered about with some general muttering about what possible necessity paint had in flying an airship; however the crew dutifully went about searching the ship.

It wasn't terribly long before Admiral Featherscarf returned with just what Timmon had desired, a small tin of black paint.

"Now why exact did ya' want this, lad?"

Timmon wasted no time in explanation but rather cracked open the lid of the tin and called out, "Brattleby!"

The massive tattooed tortoise lumbered over, "Yessir?"

"Boost me up," Timmon poured a small bit of paint on his paw and smeared it, such that it covered his entire palm. Brattleby then, without question, summarily boosted his captain up with less effort it seemed than he might have lifted a feather, and from such a height, Timmon Strongtail could just reach the base of the massive triangle of canvas that was the Summerswill's sail.

Pressing his palm firmly into the sail, Timmon Strongtail left his pawprint, "Okay, Brattleby, let me down please." Once firmly back on the deck, Tim turned to his crew, "I would like all of you to do the same. This is our ship, our home in the sky, and we'll fight to defend her. I would like all of you to leave your mark on her sail.

Once more, the entirety of the crew shared the same expression, this time it was not one of puzzlement but rather of something akin to elation.

Neesa Proudleap and Norrey Diggaburrow were the first to smear their paws in black paint, and Brattleby lifted both of them at once like it was nothing. Now the small paw of a rabbit's foot and the dexterous forefoot of a squirrel accompanied Timmon's pawprint. Admiral Featherscarf elected to instead dip a number of his primary flight feathers in the paint and streak his feathers on the sail.

One by one, all of Timmon's crew took part, and by the end, the sail of the airship Summerswill was a collage of footprints, pawprints, and feathermarks.

"We're a family, and if when we fly, this sail will be that bond. Any new crew member we may take up may make his or her own mark, agreed?" The chorus of "Ayes!" resounded around the valley.

"Then let's fly!" Timmon hopped up the bulkhead as quick as he could and took hold of the wheel. There was a hustle and bustle of motion about the deck of the airship Summerswill as all creatures of the crew went about their duties. The admiral took up his place at the prow, as first mate, hollering orders left and right and waving his taproot walking stick. Neesa, Norrey, and a sparrow named Cattatch Dartwing took up positions among the rigging. Hoory Softflight went about ensuring that all creatures were wearing their harnesses and checking that the knots were secure. Brattleby disappeared, presumably to fix something belowdeck for an early lunch. The two deckhands, a young fox named Rigger Diptail and a motherly old badger named Senna Stripeback went about removing the ground ties that were keeping the ship from going aloft for the time being, and once they had finished, Timmon felt for the first time . . .

. . . lift.

The ship was rising. An old brass lever beside the ship's wheel controlled their height, and Timmon thrust it forward; a foot pedal beneath the wheel governed their speed, and Timmon put all his weight into it, and the crew of the airship Summerswill rocketed up and up into the clouds.

Tim felt the wind whipping through his fur and tugging on Prettle Snowhelm's feather; he shut his eyes and took in the feeling of flying. He felt at that moment that he had never been happy until just then.

"Where to then?" Timmon still had not gotten over the feeling of the wind in his fur and often caught himself lost as if in a trance, standing stock still and simply enjoying of the way the wind played over him.

"Well, lad. Case you haven't noticed, we're on a war mission. Like it or not, we mean to do battle with the White-Eyed Wolf."

"I know that, Admiral."

"Lad, we've got a bit o' a problem then."

"What's that?"

"We haven't got any weapons. Cannon, blades, spears, bows, harpoons. We haven't got a thing."

"Ah." Timmon felt slightly abashed; this thought had not occurred to him ever.

"Indeed." The admiral tapped his taproot walking stick against his massive beak knowingly, and Timmon thought he saw him wink but could not be sure under his massive floppy hat.

"Well, Admiral, how do we go about procuring such an arsenal?"

"There's an old badger who lives beneath a mountain by the sea. He was the one who outfitted the Greenfleet for me way back then. He's something of an engineering genius and a fantastic metalworker. If I can guess correctly, he wouldn't just throw all of that old equipment and weapons away, so being the lone friendly airship in the skies, I think he may help us."

"Then show me the way!" Timmon thrust the Summerswill higher and stepped on the pedal that governed speed. The propellers at her rear spun faster and faster to life as the ship pushed forward at greater and greater speeds.

"West, lad! West!"

"How far west is this place, Admiral?" Timmon had been behind the ship's wheel for the duration of the day and for the most part they had been running full-board straight west. It was nearing dusk now, and Tim was lost in the view. The sun was sinking into the horizon and was the deepest shade of crimson that it looked as though it was bleeding. Beyond the dying light, at the corners of his vision, Timmon could see the first stars like specks of candlelight winking into existence amid a bruise of purples and pinks.

"Not much farther now, lad. When we can smell the sea, we'll have to turn back toward the ground. Let me take that wheel for ya' now. You've been steering all day."

"Not that difficult when we're just going straight, I'm learning," Timmon said, winking.

"Nah, I s'pose not. Still though, go wander among the crew, take in the view, get a bite 'ter eat. It'll be good for them n' you." The admiral reached for the ship's wheel, not aggressively, but assertively.

"You know best." Timmon smiled, outwardly and inwardly.

"N' lad?"

"Yes?"

"That little stunt with the paint you played today. Listen, that was a beautiful thing, n' I saw it in the crew's eyes. You were meant for this, Captain." For the first time since Timmon had met the old vulture, this former admiral of the Greenfleet, he felt a touch of true friendship in his voice, something akin to warm admiration, and it meant more than anything to Tim.

"Thank you, sir."

"Yer' welcome, Captain." Admiral Featherscarf took the ship's wheel from Captain Strongtail.

Timmon was turning to walk back down to the deck and thinking of food; he was starved after the longest day he could remember having when he thought of something and rounded. He clutched his blackwood staff close, thinking at the same time of home, and of the engraving of the ocean on the ship's lock belowdeck.

"Admiral, what does the ocean smell like?"

The admiral thought for a moment, absentmindedly working the wheel back and forth before he finally said, "It smells like beauty, Tim. Beauty."

Timmon smiled.

Timmon found himself belowdeck a few minutes later; he paused only to marvel at the view from over the edge of the Summerswill's railing. He had never imagined that there was a space between the stars and the clouds, and that looking down at them would be so much like looking at the amorphous shapes of unleavened bread like his mother used to make in the oven of the family longboat. It had been some time since he had thought of home in that way, and doing so now, he realized that that had never been home, merely a place he lived. The sky was his home now, and he loved it already.

Belowdeck he found the majority of his crew. Though some were conspicuously absent, he imagined they were simply topside. Neesa had not left the rigging all day, and Timmon could only imagine the enormity of the feeling of clinging to the rope ladders and sitting in the crow's nest. He could not wait to try that for himself. Hoory was also absent, though Timmon could not imagine where he could be or what he would be doing, but it made no matter to him; he had made up his mind to be a mindful but lenient captain, not a slave driver.

"Hello, everyone!" They had not noticed him enter, and most of them had their faces buried in bowls of Brattleby's famous leek and lentil soup. Rigger was the first to look up and waved an excited arm in the air, soup still dripping from his long snout.

"Our fearless captain! Isn't this wonderful?" He was fairly bouncing with excitement, and Brattleby put an oven-mitted claw on either shoulder from behind him to stop him jostling the table so much; dishes and glasses and utensils were rattling quite a lot.

"Now, now, youn' fox. We got a lot o' flyin', a lot o' work, and a lot o' hardships still ahead of us. Let's not get ahead o' ourselves jus' yet." Brattleby patted Rigger on the shoulder reassuringly; the young fox looked visibly deflated. Tim rounded the table and patted him on the shoulder as well.

"It's the greatest feeling ever, isn't it?" The young fox looked up at Timmon as he said this, and a wide-eyed grin that was large enough to rival the crescent moon split his face from ear to ear.

Timmon turned to the other assembled crew around the table. Cattatch Dartwing, Senna Stripeback, Isaac Southwinter, and Norrey Diggaburrow were all assembled, eating heartily. Isaac, however, was doing so by simply dipping his entire head and the majority of his neck into the bowl. He at least had removed his tricornered hat, which sat next to the bowl. Norrey noticed Timmon looking closely at this spectacle and said simply, "Yeah, well, Senna tried to discourage him doin' that. Wif' a wooden spoon no less. But he just honked real loud and kept doin' it. So we've been tryin' to ignore it. Don't bother me none."

Timmon, at the thought of this great badger beating his navigator about the head and neck with a wooden spoon, laughed so loud he thought he heard utensils clink. At the sound of this, Isaac Southwinter came up from his soup bowl, presumably to figure out what the noise was or for air.

"Honk?"

"You can eat your soup however you want, my friend. Long as it doesn't interfere with your navigation skills. Speaking of which, do you know where we're headed?" Isaac simply pointed with his wing, not removing his head from his bowl.

"Well, I'll be." Brattleby produced a compass from his stove top. "He point'd wes'."

"Geese know directions. But I believe we're getting sidetracked. I'm sure you're hungry, honey. What would you like?" Senna began to rise. Brattleby put a hand on her and said,

"No, no, no, lass. S' my kitch'n. I'll do the din'r gettin'. Wha's yer pref'rance lad?" Brattleby began to bustle about his kitchen as only a muscle-bound tortoise can. The kitchen was a modest thing; it was much longer than it was wide, and the center of the room was dominated by a long dining table lined with squat wooden benches hewn from halved logs. At the far end of the kitchen there was a low brick oven for baking and a squat fire pit for cooking over with a vent above each that fed steam to the propeller at the rear of the ship. It was lit from above by an ancient iron candelabra and a staircase about halfway down the dining room led down to the sleeping quarters, which until just recently had been the dining room of the Inn of the Rising Sun. Brattleby retrieved a deep bowl of his leek and lentil soup and hunk of hard bread larger than Timmon's head. "Sit, lad! Sit! Sit!" Brattleby placed the bowl and bread gingerly at the table between Rigger and Cattatch as it was quite close to overflowing. Timmon obliged him and sat, taking up a wooden soup spoon and sipping gently at the broth before he realized how hungry he really was and dove right in, soaking torn off chunks of bread for a moment and then sucking the juice from them.

"Lovely," Cattatch mused, smirking in that way that birds have. "So, fearless leader, where are we bound again?"

Timmon managed to speak through mouthful of food, "West, to the sea. Beneath a great mountain is a badger who once forged artillery and mechanisms for the Greenfleet. He's an old friend of the admiral, and we need weapons for this endeavor to have."

"Any chance of success," Cattatch cut Timmon off.

"Be nice, Cattatch. He is your captain." Senna was indignant, "And I'm looking forward to seeing my son again." Timmon almost choked on his food but managed to instead force the cough into his nose, which stung so badly his eyes began to water furiously.

Timmon managed to choke out, "Son?"

"Oh, yes! He's a brilliant boy with all of his metal toys. He does love them so. Why do you think I came along? I would dearly love to see my Mutter. He never visits anymore. Oh, and he'll be so excited to have you lads and lassies around for him to build toys for again!"

"Tum-te-tum-te-tee! Hello, all, I do hope that is my favorite leek and lentil soup I smell." Hoory descended the stairs to the kitchen, talons clicking on the wood, his beak clacking in anticipation of the supper to be had.

"It is ol' bird!" Brattleby immediately set about preparing a bowl of soup and a hunk of bread for Hoory Softflight. At that moment Isaac Southwinter popped his head out of his soup where it had been for some time by now and managed to speak through the soup still in his mouth.

"Mutter Stripeback is one of the most renowned smiths ever, Captain. Honk!" He plunged his head and neck back in his soup bowl which Brattleby began to refill with a ladle, never minding that Isaac's head was still in the bowl.

"Drinks lik' a fish, this'n."

"Okay! A moment, please?" Timmon was getting quite frustrated at this point and stood.

"Hmm?" said Hoory.

"Why was I the only one to not know this? I am the captain."

"You never asked." Admiral Featherscarf emerged at the foot of the stairs, the banging of his taproot walking stick had escaped Timmon in his frustration, and he had not heard the admiral approach.

"I-I-I, um. Well, no, I didn't. Can I be told these little details from now on though? Please?"

Isaac removed his head from his soup once again, "You're the captain. We're there, by the way, honk!"

"Huh?" Timmon was perplexed. Isaac waddled from the table, placing his tricornered hat on as he did so, and climbed the stairs, which Timmon had not realized until this point, geese are not made to climb stairs. They, as any creature has known a goose knows, refuse to stand with both feet on a step and suffice to extend their long, long necks the entire length of the stairs and waddle their bodies back and forth, one foot to a step, back and forth, their wide bellies gelatinously slapping the edge of each step as they climb. Timmon stifled a chuckle on his way to return to the deck.

"Oi! I smell the sea!" Neesa was at the helm and waved for Timmon to come take the wheel. Timmon didn't move, merely took in the scent of the ocean as they drifted down through the clouds. The sound of waves crashing on stone in torrents was intoxicating, and all through the air was a mist unlike any he had ever felt before. It did smell like beauty after all.

The Summerswill descended smoothly. Timmon Strongtail was not at the helm, but rather Admiral Featherscarf; Timmon was still inexperienced at piloting, and it was one thing to fly straight when in the air or to take off at a rapid pace straight up. Landing safely was a different matter, and landing in the water was far safer, though Tim much preferred to enjoy the descent, and if truth be told, he was so fascinated by the ocean that he may have crashed and was just as happy to have the admiral pilot them into a descent.

The day was swiftly dying, and only a thin line of orange and gold remained on the horizon. The sun had sank into the ocean once more to be reborn in the east on the coming day. It was true what his grandfather told him, the setting ocean was a vast and glorious thing, an endless vision of water that absorbed everything. The whitecaps in the growing light of the moon were silver and innumerable. They crashed on the rocky coast with deafening boom after deafening boom; it was ceaseless, and Timmon could not have gotten enough of watching the water on the rocks and staring into the ocean if he lived for an eternity.

To stern, rising like a massive fist, was a mountain of eroded stone, pock-marked by innumerable years of salt water and wind. The lichen that coated nearly its entire surface reflected in the moonlight and made it look as though it were soft as any bed, though just under the surface it was forged of seastone and was a treacherous thing. The admiral steered well clear of the mountain and brought the Summerswill around in a wide arc, settling her down on the ocean current as gently as one would lay an otter pup to sleep after a long day. There was only a soft crash of waves as the hull broke the surface of the water, and the fish-fin wings at the sides of the ship rose gently as the hull sank to proper depth. The rear propeller itself submerged almost completely, and only the bare tips of the blades could be seen rising above the ocean waves as it turned.

"We're here," the admiral called. "Cap'n, when I give the word slide the wheels o' the lock out o' sync or we'll continue on into the rocks. Proudleap, weigh anchor, the winch is por' side, a ways apart from the main mast."

Timmon slid below deck into the lock chamber, waiting patiently for the admiral to call.

"Now, Cap'n!"

Tim threw all of his weight into the outer wheel of the lock, gripping it by the lightning bolt and the carved plains, sliding the outer wheel a single notch to the left. All at once the light from the silverstone died, the Summerswill slowed to a crawl, then completely, then simply bobbed with the motion of the sea calmly.

There was a crash and a scream of twisting like a taut rope coming undone too quickly, followed by a furious rattle of chain links as the anchor dropped.

"Slowly, Proudleap! Slowly!"

"I'm sorry! It slipped!"

Timmon Strongtail emerged above deck, blackwood staff in hand, and noticed that it was glowing slightly. He retreated a few steps back into the stairwell of the ship's lock chamber and looked closer. In the ebbing flow of images, he could clearly make out the form of the Summerswill, flying quickly from the motion of the main mast's banner, its sail taut and its propeller spinning furiously. He noticed then that it was not the ship he was aboard now, not exactly. Her hull had been enforced with what looked like iron banding, and her prow was less of a wooden masthead and more of a battering ram, resplendent with iron plating. Cannons now broke the threshold of the moorings, dozens of them.

It was then that he noticed something far beyond the image of his ship, something dark, a floating shape that looked less like a regal bird, and more like a leather-winged bat, something gaunt and dangerous, something terrible.

"Cap'n!"

"Coming!" Tim took the steps two at a time and burst on the deck, full of excitement. "Well, let's get to it! Where is your son, Senna?"

The massive badger lumbered up from the kitchens. "I'll call him. Hallooo! Honeyy?"

Time passed and not a one of the crew said a word. Searching the darkness for any sign of the badger smith. Minutes turned into an hour, and the last vestiges of the sun died; and with those minutes the moon rose, a massive silver crescent smile, dotted all around by blinking stars. One by one the crew retired to the kitchen or further below to their quarters to prepare for bed or idly pass the time munching on hard bread and what was left of the leek and lentil soup.

Before the second hour had passed, it was only Captain Timmon Strongtail and the old badger mother, Senna Stripeback, on deck watching the waves and savoring the sea spray on their faces.

Senna finally broke the silence, "Perhaps he's moved on. He never did stay in one place for long after the eagles left the skies for the lifting of kinder winds. Too dangerous."

"No, look." There in the distance, bobbing among the waves was a dinghy. At its prow hung a small golden lamp, breaking the silver foam lines of the whitecaps. Aboard was a figure to rival Brattleby's massive bulk, he wore a brown burlap tunic; his hood was up, and he barely fit the boat he was rowing. Timmon peered closer into the darkness, trying to see beneath the darkness that his hood shed.

"Hallooo!"

"Hi, Mom!"

Mutter Stripeback cut a massive figure. He was at least three heads taller than Timmon when he hauled his bulk over the side of the Summerswill and stood. Under his burlap cloak he wore a tunic of studded leather, crisscrossed with at least a dozen belts, all bearing dirks of every shape and size; and on his hip he wore a massive mace that's head was wickedly spiked and easily larger than Timmon's own head. When he dropped his head, it was plain that he had seen his fair share of combat; he was riddled with old scars where his fur had never grown back including one particularly impressive one that ran from one ear down his face and to the nape of his neck. Timmon was simply dumbstruck at how physically massive this creature was and how many weapons he had on him.

"Hi, Mom!"

Senna Stripeback rushed to embrace her son it what could only be described as a bear hug. She was nowhere near as large as her son, but she was still quite large. When she finally broke the embrace, after what seemed like several long minutes, she held him at arms length and cooed, "Oh, my sweet baby, I have truly missed you."

"Ah, I missed you too, ma. what brings you out here, in an airship no less? I haven't seen one aloft in I don't know how many years. And who's the otter?"

"Oh, honey, this is Timmon. He's our captain!"

"He is your captain. You're joking right, ma? Where's Wattle hiding?"

"I'm here, lug. You're big s' ever I see." The admiral arrived on deck along with Hoory Softflight and Neesa Proudleap, who had her rapier drawn, clearly concerned about the crashing and banging of Mutter Stripeback boarding the ship, though she grew pale, and her lip began to quiver when she saw the size of her foe.

"S'all right, little squirrel, I ain't gonna hurt you. Wattle, what's this about this little 'un being the captain of the first airship I seen in ages?" The massive badger crossed his arms and smiled, looking Timmon up and down.

"This, Mutter, is Timmon Strongtail. Miter's grandson. He, ahem, solved the ship's lock."

"Did he now, well, my apologies, little 'un. What can I do you for, you're all an awful long way from home."

Timmon finally mustered the strength to speak, offended as he was, and he stamped his blackwood staff into the deck for emphasis, "We need you to outfit this ship for battle. We're going to take on the White-Eyed Wolf. Please."

"The Wolf, eh? You've got yourself a deal. I've had a bone to pick with him for ages, ain't had nothin' to do with these hands since the eagles left and he came along. But come inside all of you. I'll ferry you over one at a time. I'll show you what I got." He waved an arm over the side of the Summerswill and leaped down into his dinghy.

Mutter Stripeback lived in a cavern hidden from view by an outcrop of rock. The entrance was perfectly shielded from view by an inlet that twisted into the underside of the mountain. Its location made it completely hidden, but it made entering and exiting via dinghy dangerous. More than once Timmon thought for sure that they would smash into the rocks, and while he himself would have no trouble swimming, he was unaccustomed to water this choppy; and he feared for his new crew. Once inside, however, they found Mutter's cave to be extremely spacious and very dry. Its walls were coated in the same lichen that the remainder of the mountain was, and Mutter claimed that the stuff was phosphorescent and actually quite delicious when steamed over a flame or stewed in a pot.

The cave itself, after being accessed by the inlet, led to a small dock where Mutter moored their dinghy. From there they were led to an antechamber that Mutter claimed was too small, although if pressed, Timmon believed they could have fit the entire Summerswill inside. The walls had been decorated with several paintings, one of Senna Stripeback, and all of the others of either skyscapes or beautifully rendered panoramic views of Mutter's home. A fire pit had been dug into the floor, and Mutter slept on a simple cot which was massive to accommodate his size. Beyond that was a massive chamber where Mutter worked. He had constructed a great forge of stone where he worked, and claimed that there were a myriad of mazelike tunnels beyond that were rich with iron ore where he mined the metal that he worked with, which was why he had chosen this fist-shaped mountain to make his new home after the White-Eyed Wolf took the skies. He had vowed that he would work and forge new cannon and weapons until a creature brave enough to confront the evil in the skies came along.

The phosphorescent lichen shed a glow over everything. It was a soft teal at times, sometimes a brilliant sky blue, and at others a deep pine-green or even a purple that reminded Tim of the sunset he had just witnessed from the skies. The glow made everything ethereal, and it was not until Mutter lit a fire in the pit in his living quarters that the glow subsided, and it seemed things became real again.

"I got a menagerie of cannon. Some'll fit your loupes, others may not. I have grounding harpoons big enough to attach one airship to another, and hull banding and ramming plates that'll allow you to run a ship down with sheer force alone." Mutter mused as he stewed lichen in a great cauldron for them because despite the reluctance of some, he insisted they try it.

"We need weapons for ourselves as well, Mutter. Half of these folks never raised a weapon against another living creature. Cap'n Timmon has that staff o' his, and Neesa there is deadly with a rapier. Brattleby is a fine hand in a fight, I'm sure you'll remember, but he lost that mace o' his long ago. And if we're going to be fighting these brutes paw-to-paw, we'll need armor as well." Admiral Featherscarf explained over their lichen dinner, which was actually quite delicious and had a sweet tang, not unlike horseradish, but a distinct aroma and aftertaste of mint leaf. Hoory especially enjoyed it and had three helpings despite having already eaten, and he clicked his beak happily frequently and barely spoke.

"This'll take time ladies n' gents. Best you lay low here while we work. Ain't seen the White-Eyed Wolf around these here parts for a long time, but we'd best get to work soon, just in case." Mutter took another helping of lichen and strode over to his cot to lay down, "But we ain't doin' nothing until I've had me a good rest, we start first thing in the morning."

Timmon spent that night not far from their dying fire and realized as soon as he set down his head on the rushes Mutter had provided that he was exhausted. He fell asleep almost immediately.

His dreams that night were worse than they had been. He dreamed of his longboat back home, of flames licking at the deck, and his grandfather sobbing within. Try as Timmon might, he could not make his legs move, and he could not board to save him. When he leaped into the water to swim over, he found he merely sank like a stone, and beneath the water, a single white eye leering out of the river weeds on the bottom, was a wolf. His skin hung in dregs and floated lazily about his skeletal form like a tattered rag, and he had great reaching claws that took him by the legs and held him under, pulling him ever closer to a gaping maw of yellowed crooked teeth that snapped at him from the deep . . .

Timmon woke with a start, sweat covered him and soaked his fur. The cavern had returned to its former ethereal glow, a clear green-blue, the color of the ocean. All of his crew was asleep, but rolling over he noticed that Hoory, perched on an outcrop of stone, had a single eye open. He fluffed his feathers up and his lower eyelid rose in a smile as he clicked his beak knowingly.

"Mmm, lichen. Tum-te-tum-te-tee."

Timmon tried his best to fall back to sleep but tossed and turned all night.

Timmon woke the next morning to the most awful clanging and clattering. The cavern rang with the sound of banging metal, and the echoes reverberated over and over again such that the din was nearly unbearable. Rubbing the sleep that had finally found him from his eyes, Timmon stumbled up to discern the source of the noise.

All around him the remainder of his crew were also awakened. Neesa had her paws pressed into her ears so hard that her face looked like a gooseberry about to pop between two fingers, and poor Norrey was reduced to tying his ears beneath his chin comically. Isaac Southwinter just awakened and only added to the ruckus.

"Honk! Honk! Honk! Honk! Honk!"

"Silence, goose!" The admiral was also awake.

Timmon, paws dug into his ears, wandered into the larger portion of the cavern only to be nearly beaten back by the heat. The forge was like an unbearable furnace, and because of the cave walls, it had nowhere to go; it had only been a couple of minutes, but already the entire cave felt like the crew of the Summerswill was inside a fire.

"Mutter? Mutter! Mutter!" Timmon shouted until he was nearly hoarse, only then did the great badger turn about. He was clad in a thick blacksmiths smock laden to nearly snapping its neck loop with tools.

"Ah, good! He's awake! Got somethin' fer ya." From the forge he produced what looked to Timmon like a metal centipede.

"Oh, my. What is . . . that?"

"Ah, a manica!" The admiral was genuinely excited. "That'll let ya protect yer whole body without sacrificing mobility!"

"Pardon?" Timmon was genuinely lost on the subject of arms and armor.

"Here, I'll show yer." The massive badger approached Timmon and took him by the shoulder, lifting his right arm and snapping what seemed to be a dozen buckles up and down his arm, finishing by strapping a long belt around his shoulder and tying off the whole contraption with a woven thong through his palm.

What Timmon now wore was a lobstered sleeve of iron, each plate interlocking over the next. There were no gaps in the fine metalwork, and Timmon was surprised at how little it weighed. He could move completely freely and tested this by hefting his blackwood staff and spinning it in his paw, and then behind his back, and lashing out with it to his left and right and front. A great metal spaulder rose up over his shoulder with a great fan-shaped circlet of metal that rose up beside his face to nearly its full height, but was graced with a thin vent so that when Timmon cocked his head properly he could see straight through the fan.

"This is spectacular!"

"Jealous . . ." Neesa huffed.

"Great then, let's break out the brekkist!" Mutter threw up his hands triumphantly.

"What's for breakfast?" Timmon asked, still marveling at his sleeve.

"Lichen!"

The initial days of outfitting the Summerswill for battle passed with little event. As time went on Mutter fashioned massive ribs of iron binding for the hull. These the crew attached with thick rivets that bolted through the hull and were fastened within with iron washers as large as dinner plates for solidity. The prow was fitted with what looked like a spearhead. The wooden prow mast itself was removed and replaced with an iron one, though thicker and wickedly pointed at the end. Where the figurehead should have been, the Summerswill itself had originally been without one, a great metal beak was fashioned so that the ship herself resembled a hulking bird of prey, an eagle. With this figurehead, which covered the front quarter of the ship in iron, the Summerswill would be able to use the speed that was preserved by only ribbing the hull to outmaneuver any larger vessel and ram it with its massive eagle's beak. To balance the weight of the beak, iron hulling was applied around the rear propeller of the ship, strengthening its attachment to the ship and also protecting it so that the Summerswill's means of speed might be preserved in the event of a direct hit to her stern.

The cannon loupes were expanded and fitted with protective iron shutters. The widening allowed Mutter to bastion the ship with two-dozen massive mortar cannons that fired massive iron cannon balls or shells of shrapnel to cripple an enemy ship's sails. On the top deck, Mutter placed eight harpoon rifles, four to a side. With these the crew could cripple an enemy ship by attaching the Summerswill itself to them, thereby dragging them into a perilous position or simply crippling the enemy's ability to outmaneuver the Summerswill.

Mutter also introduced the crew to a weapon he had crafted himself, something even the most experienced buccaneers had never seen. Hand cannons that fired iron bolas, attached in the middle with iron-laced cord. These rifles could be fired directly at enemy crew members where the spiraling bolas would wrap themselves about the enemy crew, whether around their legs or arms, incapacitating them completely; and the bond itself would be difficult to sever in the heat of battle due to the iron lacing in the connecting cord.

It took nearly a week and immense amounts of back-breaking labor, but there was no sign of the White-Eyed Wolf, and by the end of the week, the Summerswill was a war-eagle prepared for battle; her crew was outfitted with new weapons and armor, and they were fully prepared for their war for the skies.

Timmon thought long and hard throughout these days and sparred with cutlass and blackwood staff with every member of the crew whenever they had time. He was battered and bruised by the end, but he had never felt more prepared.

He could not have been more wrong.

One evening, after the crew had finished rigging the Summerswill for battle, they sat around Mutter's cavern, celebrating. Mutter and Senna had built a great fire in the pit in the living quarters and a great cauldron of stew sat boiling over it. Hoory and Brattleby served chunks of hard bread baked with chives and peppers and a center of thick melting spiced cheese. Cattatch had gone inland a ways and found a grove of apple trees and returned over the course of the day with several bushels of apples, which Senna had baked into pies with honey and cinnamon. The mood was high, and the glow from the lichen on the walls this evening was a glorious pink, mixed with the vibrant orange and reds of the fire gave the cavern a feeling of reclining within a timeless sunset. Hoory had also shown them how to burn several needles of pine with candles and formed a light incense that filled the cavern with a most fragrant aroma indeed. All were excited about their voyage, which began on the morrow, and Mutter Stripeback had began to gather his things and was joining their crew as a deckhand. Though he was reluctant to leave his forge, he had fashioned enough cannonballs, shrapnel shells, and bola shot to last them at least a year, and they could always return to refuel their arsenal.

Neesa Proudleap had broken out a flute that she had found on board the Summerswill from a time long past, and with a little dusting off and polishing, found that it worked splendidly, and the rest of the crew discovered that she could play beautifully and knew the words to a number of old ballads.

"I gave my days to the skies above,
And left behind my only love.
For innocence and hesitance she never set paw,
On a skyfaring vessel that ne'er obeyed law.
And took we tothe world above,
Though I never forgot my love.
And returned to my home,
To find that I was left alone"

"I don't like that one, Neesa," Timmon said, spooning soup from his bowl and leaning back against a cavern wall.

"It's about a brave buccaneer who sacrifices his love for the life of the skies."

"I gathered."

Hoory laid a consoling wing on Timmon's shoulder and said through bites of bread, "We all leave someone behind at some point, Tim. If they want no part of our dreams, then they're best left out of them. Only someone who'll see you through every thick and every thin is truly worth your whole heart."

"I suppose," Timmon swallowed another mouthful of Brattleby's savory soup, "but, what about those who cannot come even if they want to?" His thoughts were of his grandfather back on his longboat.

"If they've lived their lives to the fullest, and they truly do have all their love for you, as I'm sure he does," Hoory winked at this, for he knew of Timmon's grandfather back home. "Then they will want you to experience your own dreams."

"I see. Play another one, Neesa. A happier one, please?"

"Here goes."

The next morning Timmon and the others boarded the Summerswill, strapping Mutter's dinghy to the port side of the hull in case they ever needed it again or returned to the Glowing Caverns, as they had come to call them. All of their weapons and armor they stowed in the crew quarters, and though it took much more time than expected, they managed to ferry all of the cannonballs and shells onto the ship and stow them in the gunnery on brass fittings that Mutter called "monkeys."

Lastly, the crew broke out their small can of paint and asked Mutter if he would affix his pawprint to the base of the sail as they had all done. He saw no objection and was visibly honored to be included in such a festive ritual as this. He smeared his massive badger claw with paint and pressed it into the sailcloth as they had all done.

It was nearing late-morning when the crew was entirely prepared for flight. The sun was nearing its apex in the sky, and for once the seas surrounding the Glowing Caverns had calmed. The waves themselves were shallow and infrequent, and for once the churning seas did not appear dark and near-black but reflected the sun in a way that the golden whitecaps gave way to a soft teal-green. The breeze that blew over the water was fragrant with the smells of the ocean, and Timmon took it in once more before the Summerswill took flight, standing at the prow of the ship, arm strapped from wrist to shoulder in iron, blackwood staff in hand, Prettle Snowhelm's feather flapping in the breeze.

"You all righ' lad?" Brattleby had come upon Tim from behind, shoulders clasped in iron pauldrons and a thick gorget necklacing his throat.

"Yes. Never better."

"The adm'ral wants to know when we'll be takin' off."

"Right now." Timmon turned on his heel and marched up to the helm of the Summerswill, taking one last look down at the deck where the crew stared up at him with expectant eyes, waiting for their orders. "Isaac, set a course east. Admiral, at the prow, I want you watching the skies. Neesa, Norry, Cattatch, weigh anchor and unfurl the sails. Hoory, check the ties off. Brattleby, you're on standby for orders. Rigger, to me. Senna and Mutter, ready the cannons and harpoons, I want to be ready for anything. Folks, here we go!"

Once aloft and reaching great speeds, with Captain Timmon Strongtail at the helm, the Summerswill hit a patch of rainclouds. Nothing too hazardous, just clouds of a deep slate gray laden to bursting with water. Timmon could feel the ships helm jostle back and forth as they sped through the clouds, the wings and sail becoming peppered with rain; but they were wrought of oiled sailcloth, and coated in beeswax besides, and he did not fear them soaking. These clouds were thicker than others, and he could feel the foot peddle jiggle as well under the pressure he was applying. Admiral Wattle Featherscarf ascended to the helm, his floppy hat pulled low, and the banded banners adorning his head were sodden and limp; his hats feather hung low and was plastered to his wrinkled neck. He had donned a long, gray duster, much the color of the rainclouds.

"Car'ful aroun' these clouds, lad. They can be trech'rous. Though I don' think you'll have any prob'lems. These 'uns are small things."

"I will, Admiral. Wet enough yet?" Timmon jested, though the young otter captain himself was slick with rain and fair dripping rivers, his fur was thick and made for swimming, he barely noticed the rain at all.

Aside from Timmon and the admiral, the rest of the crew had gone belowdeck until they had passed through the rainclouds at Timmon's behest. All save one, Isaac Southwinter, being a goose, was enamored with water in ways that other creatures could never hope to understand and spent his time through the rainclouds circling the deck at a full sprint, beating his wings on his chest and honking at the top of his lungs. It was quite a silly sight.

"Where do you suggest we start, Admiral?" Timmon asked that evening. Timmon had taken the captain's quarters beneath the helm; it had not been his idea; he had wished to sleep in the crews quarters with his friends, but the rest of the crew, most insistently the admiral, had adamantly assured him that they wished him to sleep in the captain's quarters as befitted him. The quarters were built of black oak, a rare wood that was as its name suggested, black. However, unlike blackwood, which was true black, black oak was veined in a rich red-orange, and in the sunlight these veins would glitter in a most wondrous way. All of the furnishings, the captain's dresser, his end tables, bookcase, four-post bed, high-backed chairs, dining table, and the edges of his mirror were all made of black oak. The bedsheets were of the finest red linen and had pillows stuffed with the softest cotton, and the bookcase had been left alone since last the Summerswill flew and was filled with literature on adventure, military strategy, cartography, and aeronautics; and Timmon Strongtail made a resolution to spend at least three hours each evening reading and learning at his desk beside the outwardly-domed picture window at the rear of his room. This window stretched floor-to-ceiling was banded in iron for sturdiness and, in times of battle, could now be closed with great iron shutters. Thanks to Mutter Stripeback's innovation.

It was at this desk that Timmon now sat, looking over a map of the Valleys, while Admiral Wattle Featherscarf occupied a high-backed chair, sipping some chamomile tea that Senna had graciously prepared.

"I suggest, Cap'n, that we set sail toward the south rim. That's where mos' evil creatures make their homes. It'd be our bes' place t' start."

"Are you sure? I was hoping to head east for a while, until we reach the Riverlands. I wanted to see my home one more time."

"T' show them you're a cap'n now? Tha' sounds a bit high-handed, lad. Rem'ber we're here t' free the skies." The admiral sipped his tea.

Timmon furrowed his brow at himself, thinking inwardly, "You're right, of course. I'd just hoped to see my grandfather again."

"N' you will. Think we're not comin' back from this mission?" The admiral peeked his ice-blue eyes out from under his hat, raising his eyebrows.

"Yes. No. I don't know. I'd just hoped that if we don't, at least I got to see him one more time."

"I'll settle that for 'ya. We don' go t' the Riverlands, n' that'll just give you all the more reason t' make it through this all righ'." The admiral stood, easing himself up with his taproot walking stick, his tea finished, "Sound like a plan, lad?"

"Y-y-yes. I think so."

Heading toward the door, the admiral turned and looked at Timmon straight on, his hat did not cover his piercing eyes, "Lad, 'ya need t' do better than 'I think so,' you're the cap'n, now. We need you. Your crew needs you." He looked at Timmon straight in the eyes, as deep into the young otter as he could, then lowered his head, as if ashamed, though it was simply the old vulture letting himself show through, if just a little, "Lad, I need you." He turned and exited the captain's cabin by the black oak door.

Timmon could scarcely believe what he had just heard the admiral say, and his jaw had dropped a little; his eyes were wide. He had not until now realized that this mission, that this ship, might mean something to the others, might mean more than anything to the rest of his crew. He had not realized that the simple fact that any of them had decided to accompany him meant that they were in this for the long haul, that they wanted this as badly as he did, and that he was their captain. He could not fail them. He simply could not.

With this realization he turned back to his book at hand and made up his mind to finish reading it before he would let himself sleep. On his desk was A Buccaneers Guide To Controlling Sky Position In Battle by Sitten Nightflyer, and ancient owl who had written a great many books on strategy in his time, many of which were collected on Timmon's bookshelf.

Captain Strongtail lit another candle to see by and took a quick glance out of his floor-to-ceiling window at the tops of the clouds beneath them, lit by the silver moonlight like a field of glittering cotton blossoms beneath the Summerswill.

He finished three books before he let himself sleep, and by then it was almost dawn, and time for the captain to take the helm.

By the next day they had reached the small mountain under which the Summerswill had been dry-docked when it was still the Inn of the Rising Sun. Off in the distance they could just make out the spire of the Eyriepeak, topped with the glimmering bastions and towers that the Eagles had once called home, though still bright and beautiful; even from a distance it was clear that the castle atop the peak had become overgrown with scrubgrass and sunken in snow with disuse. The whole of it seemed hollow, broken somehow, and it made Timmon's heart sink to look at it.

From here the crew of the Summerswill was to turn south, toward the Crag, and the lands where the viler creatures of the Valleys made their homes. Their plan, at least until that point, was to fly close to these lands, and make "an appearance." With a little luck, they would be seen by someone, and with time this message might be relayed to the White-Eyed Wolf. This plan, as the admiral and Captain Strongtail had discussed, might draw the Sky-Skinner out into the open into territory that the crew of the Summerswill would be more familiar with. It was a bold plan, though it left a lot of room for error.

What if the Sky-Skinner was accompanied by other sky pirate ships?

What if the White-Eyed Wolf did not take the bait?

What if they flew too close and were drawn into a fight in unfamiliar skies?

What if they didn't fly close enough?

All of this weighed on Timmon Strongtail's mind. He was sullen most of that day and spent his time merely steering the ship this way and that, aiming south but tacking through onrushing winds from the south. While his crew went about their duties merrily, with high-hearts to the tune of Neesa Proudleap's fluting and song, Timmon was content to merely watch. These thoughts weighed on his mind alone, and Timmon made up his mind to keep it that way; he did not want his crew's morale in jeopardy.

So went the Summerswill's second day out of the Glowing Caverns.

"I knew an otter strong as steel,
Who knew the skies so well,
That all the winds were his heartbeat,
His breath the Summerswill.
He took command on a fateful day,
And took the Wolf by throat,
And freed the skies for all to come,
This history's been wrote."

"I wrote that song for you, Captain."

"Thank you, Neesa, it's very beautiful." Timmon was still quiet, his mind ponderous as his eagle's feather played out behind him in the wind.

"I know it'll be played in every inn and hall someday because we all believe you'll make it true."

"I hope so, Neesa. I hope so."

Captain Strongtail was eating a supper of grilled onions and boiled turnips in the dining room when Cattatch Dartwing hopped up to him.

"Cap'n, can I have a quick word?" The sparrow didn't wait for a response but sat down across from him. The only other creature at the table was Rigger Diptail, and having sanded and oiled the deck that day, was much too sore and tired to pay much attention to their conversation, and Brattleby puttered around the kitchen, dicing vegetables and roots for a stew, humming merrily to himself.

"Of course, what can I do for you?" Timmon didn't stray from his meal, slicing into a turnip with his knife and shoveling it into his mouth; he had a long day himself and was also quite famished.

"Well, I come from a nest of sparrows. A lot of us to a tree. We learn from one another you see?"

"I do. What's this all about, Cattatch?" Timmon took a sip of berry juice from his tankard, wiping his mouth with the back of his paw.

"Well, sir. I saw a group of crows today. From my perch at the crow's nest ironically. Well, we grow up knowing that crows are inherently not good birds to be around. I wonder if the White-Eyed Wolf has spies?" Cattatch fidgeted nervously, or normally, Timmon wasn't quite sure; he had never known a sparrow before, and Cattatch had always seemed a little twitchy to himself, not that it was a bad thing.

"I wouldn't put it past him, Cattatch. How many did you see?"

"Three or four, sir, in the morning. Then about six this afternoon." More fidgeting.

"Okay," Timmon thought for a moment, "don't tell anyone else about this, Cattatch. But I want you up in that crow's nest all day tomorrow. I'll have Neesa bring you food and drink so you need not come down. Keep a sharp eye, and you only come down if you see anything suspicious, and only to tell me and me alone. Immediately, you understand?"

"Yes, Captain!" Cattatch's head bounced up and down in assent so quickly that it blurred.

"Good, now get something to eat, and don't worry about a thing. Rest well tonight." Timmon picked up his plate and set it in the stone sink that Brattleby washed the dishes in with a clatter, picked up his blackwood staff in his paw, which hummed and glowed at his touch, and turned to Cattatch once more before leaving. "Be alert, none of us knows what's out there waiting for us. And be careful."

"Aye, aye!"

Timmon sat in his cabin that evening. Before him was a book called Creatures of the World by a one Ittin Warrenlife. The book was a compilation of every type of creature who lived in and roamed the world. He had not perused the majority of the book but had turned immediately to "Crows." It read as such:

Crows, while often creatures who flock, a group of which is called a "murder," can also be very solitary creatures. They delight in the acquiescence of objects of beauty. Their diet consists mostly of carrion, though they have been known to suffice on other diets when carrion is scarce. They are nonmigratory and tend to find a home area where they are comfortable or where food is abundant. In interactions with other creatures, they are often used as messengers or as observationists. These interactions are often fueled by a give-and-take relationship, where the crow or crows provide a service as lookouts, messengers, or parcel carriers and are given food or coveted objects for their services. Often, crows associate with other "undesirables" such as ferrets, stoats, weasels, rats, raccoons, ravens, vultures, coyotes, foxes, snakes, and wolves.

The last word bore a hole through Timmon. Wolves. He stared and stared at it until he thought the page before him might burst into flame; he was so intent. Without another second's pause, he turned to "Wolves" and read:

Wolves are known to be both solitary and move in groups, called "packs." A wolf has a sole desire, and that is obtaining food and procreating. When in a pack environment, there is a single wolf who is granted the right to first food and the right to mate; this wolf is known as the "alpha." An alpha female is also present in every pack. The antithesis of the alpha male is the "omega" male, who in concordance is the last to eat and is never allowed to mate. This wolf, in lean times, often dies of starvation. In a pack environment, wolves rarely, if ever, associate with other creatures, though solitary wolves will often associate with other "undesirables" such as ferrets, stoats, weasels, rats, raccoons, ravens, crows, vultures, coyotes, foxes, and snakes.

Timmon was struck. He quickly grabbed his cloak (for it was quite cold that evening) off of his coat rack and his blackwood staff and nearly tore the black oak door off of its hinges in his hurry to leave the room.

Once on deck he stepped quickly to the first creature he saw, who as it happened was Norrey Diggaburrow, who was at the central hub of the Summerswill checking the knots to the crew's tie offs with deft diligent hands. He too was wearing a cloak, and with the hood pulled up, Timmon would not have known who he was except that Norrey had cut small holes so that his great ears might poke through the top.

When Timmon shouted his name, Norrey whirled on the spot, nearly tripping himself on his very large feet and saluted with a fist across his heart,

"Cap'n, what can I help you wif'?"

"Where is the admiral, Norrey? I need to speak with him!" Timmon fairly shouted at the hare and suddenly wished he hadn't because tears pecked at the corners of the hare's eyes, and Timmon realized he had scared him.

"I-I-I, uh, I 'fink he's up at the helm, Cap'n." He almost sobbed this.

"Norrey, look, I'm sorry. I'm under a lot of stress. I didn't mean to shout, you're doing a wonderful job.

"'Fank you, sir!" Norrey brightened a little.

"Carry on and thank you." Cloak swirling about him, Timmon ascended to the helm when he did indeed find the old vulture, slowly tacking the ship back and forth through the continued wind and cold.

"Ah, Cap'n. What can I do for 'ya?" Wattle Featherscarf seemed quite content, perhaps because he was happy to be back at sail in the sky or perhaps because he had just eaten a hearty plate of Brattleby's apple-crisp with cream.

"Admiral, I need to know what you know about crows."

"Crows? Ah, I'm not fond o' 'em. Nasty little creatures, them. Why do 'ya ask, Cap'n?"

"I read in a book that vultures associate with crows, is that true?"

"Tha' wouldn' be Creatures o' the Worl' would it, lad?" the admiral asked, winking.

"Why, yes. It would." Timmon felt a little rocked that the admiral had just guessed the book he had been reading.

"Lad, tha' book is a book o' judgments abou' creatures. I will say tha' a lot o' the generalities are true, but 'ya can't put faith in the idea tha' all creatures o' one type is all the same. Yes, I know a lot o' vult'rs who associate wit' crows, but I ain't one o' 'em. Now I can tell 'ya, crows do work for other nasty creatures, at least lots o' 'em do. There's some nice crows out there too, I s'pose. Why, again do 'ya ask?"

"Cattatch spotted a number of crows today. Two or three in the morning, I don't remember, and five or six in the afternoon."

"Well, tha' ain't nothin' to get your hackles raised over, Cap'n. But all the same, keep a sharp eye out. Jus' don' get lost in profilin' a creature 'cus o' what he is, lad. Dangerous business. We got a nice youn' fox on board, well as me, and he's a nice youn' feller. You don' judge him do 'ya?"

"Well, no. I like Rigger."

"I do too. Cap'n has to keep a level head, lad. 'Member tha'. Now go on, get some sleep, I got the helm, I'll wake 'ya if'n I need 'ya." Wattle gave him a large smile and went on tacking the wheel.

Captain Strongtail retired to his cabin that night with a lot to think on.

The next morning, Timmon awoke with a start. He had been dreaming again. The Wolf had been in his dreams, as he always was, only this time he had seemed clearer and more vivid where in the past he had seemed a shadowy figure or a ghostly visage. This time, Timmon had been able to make out the lines of color in his iris, the shades of gray counter to the dead white and hazy pearl, all surrounding that pupil that had been the darkest black that Timmon had ever known, blacker than midnight or the bottom of the deepest lake. He had seen his family's longboat, seen them sitting around the hearth fire, warm and at peace, and then seen the worry and the fear line their faces as they slowly realized his absence. The hearth fire had grown and grown until it was a raging inferno until it consumed their boat and spread to the rushes at riverside; and before too long the entire surface of the river, the entire forest and grasslands beyond, was aflame with fire the color of blood.

In desperation Timmon leaped from bed, the linen sheets cast all around the room in his haste, and he ripped his blackwood staff from its place on his wall, hanging where a great warrior's sword must have once been on display. He sat on the edge of his bed and peered into its depths, hoping and wishing for a vision, for the Heart-of-Gold inlay to show him something, anything. For the first time he had ever known, his grandfather's blackwood staff was simply that, black. Dark and deep like the pupil of the White-Eyed Wolf had been in his dream.

At once, like an explosion, the staff burst into gold streams, swirling and dancing like fire, as if the staff itself was ablaze with golden flames. It stayed this way for several minutes as tears came unbidden to Timmon's eyes, and he wept openly, never tearing his gaze from the staff in his paws. He wept and wept, his tears streaming down his face and dripping in rivers onto the staff, but even his tears did nothing to quench the flames that licked out in Heart-of-Gold. All at once again, the flames ceased, and the staff was dark again.

Then, little by little, like ripples in a limpid pond expanding from a thrown pebble, another picture began to take shape. First a pole, then the shallow sides of a hull, and the ferry cabin, and the limp, triangular sail, and deck fire pit . . .

. . . of the Strongtail longboat.

Someone rapped on his door and entered. Admiral Wattle Featherscarf strode into the room, supporting himself with his taproot walking stick, eyes agleam with merriment.

"We're almost there, lad. Your turn a' the helm."

"Turn us around."

"W-w-wha'? Where're we goin', lad?"

"Home."

It took the crew of the Summerswill nearly two days to reach the Riverlands. They arrived in the wee hours of the morning on the second day before the sun had yet risen from its resting place beneath the rising sea. In these two days, Captain Strongtail showed what his colors were under desperation. He did not sleep; he staunchly refused to eat, and when offered even a small glass of berry juice to keep his strength, he refused that too. They Summerswill flew through clear skies and clouds through a patch of rain so fierce that the entire crew went belowdecks, even Isaac who was so fond of rain. Timmon Strongtail stayed at the helm through it all, his teeth gritted, his foot on the acceleration pedal with all of his weight, eagle feather whipping out behind him as if still a part of the great Prettle Snowhelm in all the glory of flight.

"Captain, perhaps a different perspective on the situation might offer some answers or at least allow you a glimpse of the fuller picture?" Hoory Softflight rarely left his captain's side; he feared for him and worried endlessly. "Dreams are very interpretive ideals, Captain. They can be seen from a multitude of different perspectives depending on expert opinion or casual observation. They may be the windows into our subconscious, yes. Although they can also be twisted by our feelings."

"Are you an expert, Mr. Softflight?"

"Hoory, please, Captain." Hoory clicked his beak worriedly; his eyes were narrowed with concern, and he polished his monocle constantly, a nervous habit.

"Hoory, are you an expert?"

"Not in the study of dreams, Captain, no, I am not. Although, as I said they are not something that can be studied quantitatively, only qualitatively."

"Laycreature's terms, Hoory." Timmon gritted his teeth so fiercely, Hoory thought they might splinter.

"Dreams can only be studied in an interpretive sense. They cannot bc given a definitive definition."

"When I dream, Hoory, when I wake in the night, I see him."

"Hoo, Captain?"

"The Wolf. He haunts me, and the other night I saw my family's longboat aflame and my family gone, absent."

"If I may make an observation, Captain, the fact that they were absent and not in some danger, is that not a good sign?" Hoory blinked in anticipation, perhaps this was a good sign.

"Well, they were there, then the hearth fire grew and they were, I don't remember, but I saw the river afire." Timmon could scarcely remember the dream anymore; all he remembered was the terror and the horror he had felt upon waking. What he remembered clearly was the etchings in Heart-of-Gold and what it had shown him, the fire and his family's longboat. Besides that fact, his blackwood staff, his grandfather's gift, had been solid black for the last two days; he kept it beside him at the helm at all times. "The fact is, Hoory, my staff, my grandfather's staff, has remained dark ever since that morning when I saw fire and the longboat."

"Was the boat itself ablaze, did you see your family?" Hoory leaned closer.

"Well, not insomuch, no."

"Again, perhaps I am extending my reach too far, grasping at straws as it were, but perhaps this is not such an omen as you understand it to be."

"One way or the other, Hoory, we're going to the Riverlands to ease my mind at the very least." This last Timmon said, he did not truly believe. He knew in his heart what he might find, and his heart was empty and fallow at the thought. Pressed on he did, though, he pushed his ship as fast as he could toward the Riverlands.

"That's all in fairness, Captain. I shall leave you be for a time to obtain some sustenance for myself. Fly safely."

"Thank you, Hoory." Captain Strongtail pressed the accelerator as hard as he could.

The Riverlands themselves were a vast place. The entire eastern seaboard of Sylva were snaked with rivers and streams, and finding a single longboat in them from the sky would be like identifying a single dewdrop on a spiderweb coated in morning dew. When at last the Summerswill broke over the Riverlands, the clouds miraculously broke, and Timmon was able to ease the Summerswill down to a comfortable depth. He allowed the admiral to take the helm, while Senna and Cattatch managed to procure three spyglasses from some storage chamber nestled deep within the ship.

"Cattatch, I want you and Hoory flying just below the ship; use your eyes. Let me know immediately if you spy anything suspicious. Admiral, take the ship low and tack her back and forth so that we might get a look at anything and everything. Isaac, to me, break out your maps and keep track, I don't want to cover any ground twice and go in circles. Senna, please give me one of those spyglasses. Rigger and Mutter, get the other two, you two have the best eyes. The rest of you, keep a wary eye on the skies. I don't like this at all."

A chorus of "Ayes!" abounded across the deck of the airship Summerswill, and Timmon took his spyglass in paw and telescoped the brass sections out, pressing the ocule to his eye and peering back and forth over the railing of the ship, looking and looking and looking.

For several hours they perused the Riverlands. Here and there they spied a longboat, though never was it the one belonging to Timmon's family. Strangely though, every one seemed to be in disuse, and no creatures were spotted poling or fishing or braking camp. No younglings were at play; no elders were at rest. There was simply nothing as if the world had taken pause and left behind only the things that creatures had and spirited the creatures themselves away.

By midday, the crew had reported seeing about thirty longboats, all of which had been in the same state of in-between, neither mobile, nor truly docked, simply tied off at the shore and devoid of any activity or life. Timmon grew more and more worried and sick with apprehension as the day wore on. Brattleby eventually decided it was time for a meal though it was well past the time when the crew would normally sit and eat; he moved belowdecks to the kitchen to whip up some light sandwiches and butter-fried vegetables. One by one the crew went to eat, Hoory and Cattatch landing on deck and quickly descending the stairs to eat before returning and taking flight once more to search.

About an hour after Brattleby had fed the crew and offered Tim a plate laden with morsels that he did not touch, Rigger came to Timmon Strongtail, approaching quietly for he did not want to startle his captain.

"C-captain? Sir?" Rigger fidgeted nervously,; he removed the bandana that he usually wore wrapped around his head and turned it over and over in his hands restless with fear.

"Yes?"

"I thought you ought to know, not that this strikes me as completely odd, but I've been noticing something strange."

"And what's that?" Timmon dropped his spyglass from his eye with a quick flick of his paws, preparing for the worst news but also tense as a coiled snake for want of news. He whipped around on his heels so fast that Timmon nearly lost his balance and fell over the railing.

"Well, if you look there, sir, over the bulkhead at the rear . . . I-I-I thought it was a raincloud at first like the ones we went through to get here, but then I noticed that . . . well, I think it's moving."

Timmon whirled on the spot and brought his spyglass once more to his eye. There, off at a distance he couldn't gauge by sight, was a slowly drifting cloud of black. The cloud broke and reformed itself seemingly at will and fluttered just out of focus like a mirror reflection refaced in rippling water, Timmon simply did not know what to make of it. He stared and stared until Neesa approached him from behind and said simply,

"Crows."

"A cloud of crows is following us," Timmon said it as a fact; it was not a question. He lowered his spyglass and called, "Admiral! To me! Neesa take the helm, keep us on course."

"Aye!" she cried, scampering away the bells and bangles in her tail jingling loudly.

Timmon raised the spyglass to his eyes once more, looking south toward the shifting mass of crows at their stern. It was clear now what they were, Timmon could see the lighter colors of the clouds phasing in and out between the wings of thousands of crows off in the distance. The ship had slowed since they reached the Riverlands and had began their searching. So Timmon shouted up to the helm, "Neesa, take us full speed ahead!"

"Aye, aye, Captain!" Came the squirrels call from above them at the helm.

Just then Admiral Wattle Featherscarf limped up behind Timmon and demanded of Rigger Diptail, "Your spyglass! This instant, young one!" The young fox obliged quickly, thrusting the spyglass to the aged buccaneer, who snuck the ocule of the spyglass under his large hat and peered off into the distance through it. "Aye, they're crows a'right. We need 'ta set down somewhere, Tim. Southwinter! Where's the closes' large body o' water?"

"The Owl's Eye! Honk! It's south of here a little, but we can reach it before them crows do!" Isaac had waddled up at some point to see what was going on; Timmon had not noticed him until that moment.

"How do you know?" Timmon was skeptical, although he was a poor judge of distance in the sky as of yet.

"They're honk a long ways off yet. If we move full speed we can get there first." Isaac had broken out a sheaf of maps from his belt and inserted his loupe into his eye, cocking his tricornered hat far back on his head and was poring over the maps as quickly as he could.

"Admiral, take the helm, you can get us there and set us down faster." Timmon delegated other orders at a shout, waving his blackwood staff this way and that to point, "Isaac, up at the helm with the admiral. Neesa, Rigger, Norrey, to the rigging! Hoory, on deck and on point when I need you! Cattatch, to the crow's nest, now! Senna, Mutter, Brattleby, ready the cannon, we may need them!" As the other creatures rushed to their posts, Timmon sprinted to the main hub of the ship where all of the crew's tie offs were knotted and began running them to each crew member. He sprinted a pair of cords to the helm, where Isaac knotted his about his waist and did likewise with the admiral's. Neesa's, Norrey's, and Rigger's he tossed into the air for them, one at a time, and Neesa deftly caught each one and swung through the rigging to each creature, knotting them firmly about their waists. Brattleby, Senna, and Mutter were belowdecks and safe from flying off of the ship, and Hoory and Cattatch could fly if needs be; Timmon was running out of seconds. Timmon knotted his own leash last, cinching it tightly about his waist and knotting it three times to make sure.

"Hold on, you lot!" The admiral jammed his taloned foot into the acceleration pedal and spun the ship's wheel hard to the left, letting his feathers tic against the many handles as they spun past until it had turned many times, and he grabbed it firmly once again.

The Summerswill lurched like a wave on a stone, and for a full heartbeat was nearly horizontal. Timmon grabbed onto the ship's hub with both paws, his blackwood staff clenched firmly in his teeth; those in the rigging clung to their rope ladders with all of their strength. The admiral held the helm and Isaac held the admiral. Cattatch and Hoory gave small hops and spread their wings, catching the draft from the Summerswill and hovering for a moment while she righted herself; and the admiral spun the helm back into place, and the great fish-fin rudder beneath the ship righted itself. As quickly as it had happened, the crew was back on solid deck and safely nestled in the rigging.

"Here we go!" The admiral crushed whatever weight he had left into the acceleration pedal, rammed the height lever forward and the Summerswill shot up and up and up into the air betwixt the clouds and the stars once again.

Once it seemed they were halfway to the stars, Admiral Featherscarf leveled out the Summerswill once more. Soon they were catapulting forward at intense speeds, the wind whipping across the deck threatened to dislodge some of the smaller creatures, and they were forced to go belowdecks while the larger creatures came back above to check the knots in the sails and at the ship's hub, though they were useless in climbing the rigging if the Summerswill was to get to the Owl's Eye in time to avoid detection of what all assumed was a murder of the White-Eyed Wolf's henchmen; they would have to do so with speed.

Timmon chose to remain at the helm with Admiral Wattle Featherscarf and Isaac Southwinter; besides, Isaac needed another creature to help him hold down the maps he was using to guide the ship, lest they be sped away by the torrents of wind.

"How much further!?" Timmon had to shout over the roar of the wind, and when he opened his mouth wide to do so, he found he was instantly choked with rushing air and could not breath and had to choke the words out. He had not realized until then that he had been straining to breath this entire time or had been holding his breath, he couldn't tell.

"Not far!" Timmon was unclear as to whether the admiral or his navigator had spoken, but it was not punctuated with a honk, so it must have been Wattle.

Tim found himself wishing he had bothered to don his manica; light as it was, the little extra weight it provided would have helped him hold down the maps at least as he was having a horrible time catching one page or the other by the corners as they threatened to spin into the wake of the Summerswill and soon found himself also wishing that Isaac Southwinter was a little more organized with his papers.

"Hold them still, honk! I can't tell where we are!" Isaac shouted out, his long neck snaking back and forth over the maps, trying to figure out their coordinates based on their course and their speed.

"I'm sorry, hold . . ." Timmon shifted a paw to try and steady some of the other papers which were flying this way and that when the back draft caught them. They were carried off into the wind before either goose, otter, or vulture had quite noticed.

"Um, honk?" The look on Isaac's face was one of utter befuddlement. "I guess just take us down, Admiral. We'll have to see where we are from here."

Without a moments hesitation the Summerswill went into a near nose dive, shooting downward like a striking falcon. The stars above disappeared; they spanned the cloud barrier so quickly that Timmon barely glimpsed the passing of the skyward cotton fields, and an instant later they were witness to the nearly-dying light of day; and beneath them, a great gray-blue circle of lake, “The Owl’s Eye!” Timmon shouted, having recognized it immediately from when he had played there once as a pup.

“Yes, but look there!” The admiral pointed straight ahead of them with his taproot walking stick while still gripping the helm and throttling up their speed, his jacket spitting out behind him like the flicking tongue of a great lizard.

Timmon looked up, and there, racing toward them was a murder of crows that could have blocked out the sun for days with it’s passing.

“Oh, no.”

"I got this!" the admiral screamed, as they continued to speed toward the lake, flying so low over the forest of evergreen and oak that surrounded it that Timmon thought he may have been able to touch them if he'd reached out. "WOOO-HOOO!" the admiral whooped with exhilaration, much to Timmon and Isaac's surprise. Sure enough leaves and pine needles began to spit up all around the Summerswill like deep-green sea spray; they were so close to the forest canopy.

In half a moment they were over the Owl's Eye, and the admiral yanked back the height control lever with an audible grating of brass instruments; and the Summerswill, in all her bulk and beauty, dropped like a red-hulled stone.

"Get to the lock!" the admiral shot at Tim, a look of ice-blue fury and something quite like madness in his piercing eyes (his floppy hat had long since fallen off his head and hung on to his fleshy neck by a cord).

With all the speed and tenacity Timmon Strongtail could muster, he leaped the rail to the ship's deck below, rolling over his shoulder as he crash-landed into the wood. He scuttled along the deck to the stairs, and all but tumbled down them and scampered through the kitchen where the rest of the crew was holding one another for fear of crash. He moved through so quickly and in such a tumbling manner that a good many of them gasped and clutched each other, thinking that perhaps they had crashed. Just as he fell rolling into the ship's lock chamber, he heard a barely audible "Now!" from above; he grabbed hold of the closest symbol in the outer ring and, with all the strength he could muster out of panic, ripped it to one side, desynchronizing the lock and stopping the Summerswill in her tracks.

Sitting on his behind, gasping for air, Timmon gradually began to roll onto his four paws and stand, and then caught himself on the wall; he was so exhausted. Leaning on the wall as he ascended the stairs, crossed the kitchen amid silent gazes from the rest of his crew and to the deck, Timmon barely remembered the next few seconds.

On deck he realized that the admiral had managed to pull them safely into the southern estuary that flowed into the Owl's Eye lake, and that Neesa was once again, clumsily lowering the anchor. From this place, he could also see that the Summerswill was under the cover of the canopy of the forest, which stretched along the river right up to the shores of the Owl's Eye.

Kneeling on the stairs ascending to the helm, he saw the ragged figure of the admiral who only mimed a command with one feather and his beak, shhh.

Just then, the cawing, shrieking cloud cover of crows flew over their position. A writhing pool of blackness that screamed overhead like the herald of a coming doom; the beating of thousands upon thousands of wings alone ruffled every leaf and every pine needle in the forest around them, and a rain of acorns and dead branched shook free of their arboreal ancestors and clattered like a hailstorm onto the sails and deck of the Summerswill.

All went dark, and Timmon realized he had been right; they did blot out the sky after all.

Captain Strongtail had assembled his entire crew in his captain's cabin. All were present, except for Cattatch, who hopped in and out of the room sporadically, watching the canopy of pine and oak above their heads; and when he felt all was clear, he would flit out to the sky over the Owl's Eye for a quick look around. Neesa had agreed to fill him in on any particulars of this meeting, and all were comfortable with that idea; and the captain and the admiral had not wanted to leave the ship completely unattended while they met with the crew.

Timmon began, leaning heavily on his blackwood staff, his eyes to the black oak flooring, "Listen, all of you. For those of you who don't know, I had a dream. It was the strangest dream, and they've all been strange since I left home, but this one was . . . different. I had a feeling we should return to the Riverlands because I thought my family may be in danger," He paused to press his paws into his eyes, squeezing back tears, "Our mission, when all of this began was to free the skies from oppression, and I hope that's what you all signed up for. In fact I believe in my heart that is what you all believe in or you would not have joined me that day at the inn. Since long ago when the eagles left the skies for the lifting of warmer winds, the undesirables of the south, predominantly the White-Eyed Wolf, have kept the skies for themselves; and if rumor and suspicion persist and lead to truth, he'll take the lands and the seas and inland waters next. If we're going to bring about a world where creatures need not live in fear where airships whose only business is trade and transport and leisure are free to fly once more, we need to be vigilant, patient, and passionate."

This last statement brought about nods and assents from the entire crew, all simultaneously agreeing.

"I'm going south now. That murder was enough to prove that someone down there knows we're here, and it's only a matter of time before the Wolf knows, if he doesn't already. This means the Summerswill, and whoever crews her will be in great danger; and I don't want anyone coming with me who has the least bit of fear or worry in their hearts or families back home waiting for them, creatures who depend upon them, creatures who love them dearly." Timmon stood with the help of his blackwood staff, finally raising his eyes and looking around the room, at the faces of his entire crew. All had stoic, resolved but not resigned expressions on their faces.

"I want to see my family again, but for all I know they've been taken or are in danger. And I realize now that without the wolf gone from the skies, it'll never be safe for me to visit them or for them at all. So we're leaving after the ship is checked for landing damage, and who wants to stay, if not, I'll not judge you for leaving. I've said my peace then. I'll be waiting at the helm for us to fly out. Meet me there if you intend to stay. As Tim began to walk toward the door, he was blocked by a great slowly moving mass large enough to block the light from the door with its entire bulk. Timmon looked up and saw the kind face of Mutter Stripeback staring down at him, cocking his head this way and that slowly, looking his captain all over.

"I'm with you, Cap'n." He crossed a great badger paw over his heart.

"As am I." Neesa crossed her fist over her heart.

"And I." Cattatch, who had just hopped back in, spread his wing over his breast.

"I as well." Senna.

"Me too." Rigger.

"Aye, lad." Brattleby.

"Cap'n." The admiral.

"Aye, sir!" Norrey.

"I include myself in this endeavor." Hoory.

"Honk!"

Brattleby, Mutter, and the admiral checked the Summereswill, every inch of the ship, for any signs of damage incurred during their water-landing. A few sail buckles on the port, and starboard sails had frayed when the ship flew too low over the nearby treeline; but other than that, the Summerswill was as skyworthy as she had ever been, and Timmon was grateful at least for that.

Tim went himself to check the weapons deck and ensured that every cannon was securely tied and that no cannonballs had slipped off of their monkeys during the landing (which they had not) and caused any damaged rolling back and forth. He asked Mutter to acquaint him and the rest of the crew well with the bola rifles, cannon, and harpoon guns. They trained for many hours a day on these weapons though were careful never to use gunpowder for fear of causing an accidental discharge and someone getting injured or of the shot being heard by any undesirables in the area.

Indeed it took almost three days for a full look at the Summerswill. She was not a very large airship by any means. She was built to be small and quicker and have more agility than larger ships, but her crew was still small, and a full work list took some time for the crew to manage.

Timmon insisted that whatever crew members were not immediately engaged in some task that the Summerswill required, they should stay above deck and practice their combat. All of the crew learned from one another. Each took turns teaching the crew, telling what little they knew; and oftentimes, these practice sessions would turn into near-philosophical debates over the merits of certain styles of fighting as opposed to others. When these discussions began, Timmon did his best to focus the crew's attention back on their fighting practice, although this did not always work, and he sometimes found himself witnessing a heated argument between Brattleby and Mutter discussing paw-to-paw fighting and how different stances can affect the eventual outcome of the fight.

Though frustrated at first with these segues into debate, Captain Strongtail soon found himself listening very closely to what each and every member of the crew had to say, trying to pick up bits of this and that. He would go over the things he had learned that night while he sat wide awake in bed after having pored over the ancient scrolls, forgotten tomes, and the more modern books that littered the bookshelf of the captain's cabin.

He did not realize it at the time, but Timmon was growing both physically and psychologically by leaps and bounds. His muscles were growing taut and sinewy and responsive to combat stimuli, and his mind became more and more filled with vital information with every book he read.

Timmon Strongtail was not quite aware of the transformation, though his crew was. He was becoming a true captain of an airship.

On the morning of the fourth day, the crew of the airship Summerswill donned their arms and armor, and with the ship's lock engaged, the anchor was drawn in. Hoory and Cattatch flew a screen around the Summerswill as Timmon, under the guidance of the admiral, eased the Summerswill out of the inlet, out into the center of the Owl's eye, and up and away into the sky. The Summerswill flew north at first; and then, using the push and pull of the wind, veer the ship around to her port side, the port hull showing herself to the land below and turning toward the south.

Once aloft and making good course, Timmon recalled Cattatch and Hoory to the deck, though he immediately sent Cattatch to the crow's nest to keep a lookout with one of the spyglasses and gave the others to Hoory and Neesa, where they patrolled the port and starboard sides of the ship, peeking off into the distance for any sign of the murder or of anything else out of the ordinary.

"You're doin' the right thing, lad. Ya know tha', don' ya?" Admiral Wattle Featherscarf stood behind his captain and off to the left, leaning both on his taproot walking stick and the railing of the Summerswill. It had been a long couple of days, and the admiral was stiff with ache.

"I think so. I hope I am."

"Ya are."

"How can you be so sure?" Timmon idled the helm back and forth, tacking into the southern winds and quickly as he could.

"We all had fam'ly, lad. At one time. The creat'res here with you, they all got someone to protect, and if'n they don't, then this mission be somthin' they care deeply abou'."

"You really think so, Admiral?"

"I know it."

"Well then, thank you, sir. Check on the deck, will you? Make sure all is running smoothly."

"Gladly, Cap'n!" The old admiral shuffled off, his walking stick tapping every step on the way down to the deck from the helm.

Timmon Strongtail reflected on all of this as he steered the Summerswill southward. Was the admiral right, was there not a creature on board who didn't have someone to go home to? If that were so, Timmon thought he may be sick; the idea of losing a crew member on this endeavor and having to take that responsibility . . . well, Timmon was not sure he could have that weight on his shoulders no matter the good that came of it.

Tim spent the rest of the day sailing south, thinking to himself. At lunch, Senna brought him a bowl of oatmeal with chopped apples and blackberries mixed into it, topped with honey, and a cup of water. Timmon was grateful, although he did not show it or say anything; and Senna, being a wise old badger, could sense his mind was elsewhere and took no offense when Timmon did not strike up a conversation but met her simply with a "Thank you."

Timmon was still thinking when the sun sank back into the sea, out beyond the foothills and western peaks off the starboard side. He watched the deep blues of late afternoon fade into yellows and oranges, pinks and purples and reds, and though it was the most beautiful sunset, Timmon could not appreciate it.

Deep into the night they traveled, the ship's lock powering the propeller at the rear of the Summerswill to full speed; even into the wind, the crew was making fine time. Despite having his family, his quest and his visions on his mind, Captain Strongtail was vigilant in the safety of his crew. He asked almost every hour for the tie offs to be checked and was rigorous in making them go belowdeck one at a time to eat; and as long as Brattleby kept the kitchen running smoothly, which he was no slouch at, every member of the crew of the Summerswill ate three full meals a day.

Though he felt he had little time, Neesa was quick to remind Timmon that he still needed to practice. As weapons master, it was her duty to ensure that every member of the crew was at all times prepared for a fight.

"Captain, you need more practice."

"I have to fly the ship, Neesa."

"Let the admiral take a shift or two. You need to practice, and you need to sleep."

With a resigned sigh, Timmon assented. He knew she was right; she often was. He did need the practice with his blackwood staff; he would be no good to the crew as a captain if he could not face-off against the sky pirates in paw-to-paw combat.

Timmon called the admiral to the helm where the old vulture took the wheel and continued to steer their course south. Tim retrieved his blackwood staff from where it had rested beside him and would have had to retire to his cabin to fix his manica to his arm, but the entire crew now wore their armor at all times; they were always prepared.

Down on the deck, Neesa had taken an offensive stance and was awaiting the arrival of her captain. When he strode into her field of view, not yet prepared for a fight, Timmon's guard was down, and she charged him.

"Wha!" Timmon did not see the flurry of blows that came at him from Neesa's wooden practice sword, but like a flurry of hailstones they struck him everywhere. A good many were caught by his manica, proving its usefulness; but two blows caught him in the thigh, and the last blow was a stinging downward slash to his left wrist. "I wasn't ready!"

"The Wolf won't wait until you're ready, Captain."

"Did Wattle put you up to this?" Timmon rubbed his sore wrist which was already beginning to swell.

"Yep." She lunged again; this blow Timmon caught with the crook of his armored elbow, whirling around with the staff in his left paw and striking out at the backs of her knees. Neesa was a nimble fencer, and her bells jangled merrily as she danced out of the way. She wore only a modest tightly fit breastplate which left her a lot room for mobility, much like Timmon's armor.

Timmon went on the offensive now, striking out at her left foot, the right, then right again before passing the staff behind his back and switching to his right hand and swinging a wide arc at her head. Ducking just in time, Neesa jabbed forward with her rapier, a blow that Timmon bent at the knees and caught with the frilled plate that guarded his shoulder and neck.

Timmon took the momentum of the blow and slid down, balancing himself with his tail, and laying across his shoulders, he aimed a high arcing blow straight down the middle of Neesa's chest; this blow hit home,and Timmon could feel through his staff the vibrations in her breastplate. Hopping up quickly, Timmon spun behind Neesa and swung an equally hard blow across the small of her back; this blow laid her flat. Timmon danced away and readied his staff for another attack, but it was clear now that Neesa was down.

"You, are getting, better." Neesa huffed from the deck.

"You are too," Timmon smiled inwardly. "Enough for the night?"

"I yield." Timmon strode over and offered a paw to help her up which Neesa gratefully took and stood, retrieving her wooden practice rapier as she did so.

"Go get something to eat, Neesa. You were right, I do need more practice, but for now I'm going to get some sleep."

"Okay, sleep well, Captain."

"You too!" Once inside his cabin, Tim stripped off his manica, hung his blackwood staff on the wall, and took the book from his bedside that he had been reading. Before he had even managed to crack the book open, his head hit the pillow. Not even yet under the sheets, Timmon Strongtail was asleep before he knew it.

"Captain! Captain! Captain!" Timmon shot straight up, awake in a moment, being shaken by someone.

"Wha, what? What is it?" Timmon didn't have a second to rub the sleep from his eyes but grabbed up his blackwood staff and began looking around the room for where he had taken his manica off, finally noticing it was Neesa who had woken him, and he asked again, "What is it?"

"The admiral wants to see you on the helm. He says there's something you need to see." She was not saying everything, and there was a look of something in here eyes, something not unlike fear but not quite terror, Timmon thought it looked like wary-apprehension. When he picked up his manica and began the process of bucking it to his arm, little by little, she helped him with the laces and the chest strap. Timmon noticed that she too was armed; all of the crew had been wearing their armor as a precaution, but now Neesa Proudleap also carried her rapier at her side, and her paw kept flicking to its hilt, something that Timmon might have taken for a nervous habit if this hadn't been the first time he had seen her do it, something was up.

Lashing his sword belt about his waist, Timmon also buckled his cutlass in place; he was nowhere near as comfortable with a blade as he was with his staff, but the urgency with which Neesa awakened him made him think that he had better take it.

Captain Timmon Strongtail threw open the black oak door to his cabin onto the deck and was struck immediately with fear. The Summerswill had been flying all night while he slept, and they were nearing a mountain chain known as "the Mane," where beyond lay the Crag and the domain of the White-Eyed Wolf. Beyond the mountain range, Timmon saw the rising sun, and he had never seen a darker spectacle. The sun rose behind them and was the perfect color of blood-red; it seemingly gave off no light but was simply a celestial body sitting in the sky like an apple bobbing in an ocean of black and what light did reflect from it did so off of the Mane. The mountains rose like an array of bloody teeth; their peaks so sharp and steep that they looked more like a crux of pine trees than monuments of stone, red as they were. Above and beyond the Mane, he could see swarming loops of black, fidgeting, and squalling up and up in tornadoes of dark shapes before collapsing once again into the cluster beneath like a thousand flies over something dead.

"Tha's the Crag, lad." Brattleby had come up behind him while Timmon was stunned with the sight before him, "Be'ind the mountains is the Wolf."

"I never thought that there was such a place in the world."

"There is," Brattleby said simply, his own eyes transfixed by what lay before them. Without saying another word to Brattleby, Timmon ascended to the helm where Hoory Softflight and Admiral Wattle Featherscarf were both at the helm, the admiral steering and Hoory speaking plainly with him. When Timmon came upon them, they both ceased speaking and greeted him instead.

"Ah, good Captain Strongtail, I trust you've observed our near-arrival at the Mane and the Crag." Hoory, despite what lay ahead, seemed to be in as good of spirits as ever and closed his eyes in a smile at seeing Timmon ascend the steps.

"Yes, Hoory. I've noticed. What is our plan from here, Admiral?"

"Tha's not for me t' say, Cap'n. You're the cap'n after all." The admiral showed no gleam of sarcasm or stinging with in his eyes, and he seemed clearly to have been making an observation. Timmon was after all the captain of the Summerswill.

"Well, I, erm. I don't suppose I know." Timmon turned and looked once more at what lay ahead of them, and the spectacle almost took his breath away once more; the horrific sight of those red, stone teeth rising up from the ground before them looked so gaunt and terrible, and the sun behind them seemed to be winking in jest as if it knew what lay before them even if they did not or had not.

"I'm sure you need a moment to think, good captain. It is after all, a decision that may warrant a list of pros and cons, or perhaps you wish to revisit the old captain's logs and surmise how they approached such a situation?"

"No cap'n ever came this near the Crag while the Wolf was 'ere," the admiral growled, his voice like flint stones striking.

One way or another, yes, I need a moment to look at the maps to see what we need to do." Timmon was about to turn and walk back to his cabin to pore over the ancient captain's logs and examine what maps he had left after he and Isaac had lost a great number of them during their last descent when he head a shriek.

"Look out!" The cry came from the crow's nest from high up where Cattatch was posted, and it took only an instant for the reason why to make itself present. All at once, a crow the size of Timmon, tumbled over the starboard side of the Summerswill straight into Neesa, who stood near the ship's hub. It rolled to a stand near her and swatted at her with its great beetle-sheen wing and caught her in the chin; she was unprepared and off her guard for only a moment, and she staggered back against the port side railing. A moment later the crow was on her again and struck her once more; she was dazed, and this hit also caught her in the jaw, and like a rag doll, Neesa Proudleap tumbled over the side of the ship where her tie-off went taut.

In a fury that Timmon could not explain, he leaped over the railing of the helm to the deck below, and his blackwood staff was in his hands before he realized it. He crossed the space between him, and the crow in two large bounds; and before he could have thought to stop himself, he brought down a blow with the staff onto the crow's skull as hard as he could. Not ceasing his attack, his next three blows followed in quick succession at the crow's breast, each of which hit with a thick thud of a blunt object on a creature's lungs. The crow was staggered, reeling from one foot to another, its wings outstretched for balance and its head unprotected. Timmon swung one final blow that caught the crow in its great beak, and its body followed its head . . . over the railing and far through the clouds below.

"Neesa!" Timmon rushed to the railing where Neesa lay, still stunned suspended by her tie-off. Behind Tim, Mutter had grabbed the tie off leash and was hauling Neesa in by great lengths. In a moment she was near enough that Timmon Strongtail reached down and grabbed her by the shoulders of her painted vest and hauled her over the railing. He lied her down on the deck where she lay for a minute still stunned while the rest of the crew of the Summerswill gathered around. "Are you all right, Neesa?"

Her eyes rolled around to meet Timmon's, and she managed a small smile, "Guess we know what we're in for now."

Timmon was the least amused of anyone at her statement. The rest of the crew, at least those who were seasoned sailors, seemed to think of the incident with the crow as something of a baptism by fire for the new crew members; and Brattleby told Timmon later in private that the crew was quite impressed with how he had handled the crow, and it wasn't until that moment that it sunk in what he had done.

Timmon was unsure whether the crow had lived or died. He had hit it hard enough to stun it such that it was wobbling as it tried to stand, and then he had hit it again so hard that it had toppled over the edge. But they were the enemy, weren't they? If the crow had lived, he found himself wondering if it would go straight to the White-Eyed Wolf and warn him of their presence; and for that he hated the crow, and he pitied it all the same. Perhaps the crow, while falling, had regained its strength and taken flight. What if the crow had simply flown away, deciding that the Wolf's trinkets were not worth being bashed about the head so? Sitting in the kitchen, Timmon pondered all of this, and as though he could sense his captain's conflictions over his actions, Hoory came over, his talons scratching at the floorboards beneath his feet; he polished his monocle and made a show of checking his captain for wounds and the like,

"Did the crow manage to assault you with his beak, Captain?"

"No."

"What about his claws, Captain, are you wounded anywhere from his claws?"

"No."

"Are you concussed? Did you suffer a blow to the head? What is your name? What is the name of this ship? What was the name of the eagle who's feather you wear in your fur?"

"Timmon Strongtail, Summerswill, Prettle Snowhelm. I'm fine, Hoory. He didn't injure me at all." Timmon held his head in his paws in exasperation.

"Captain?"

"Yes, Hoory?" He did not remove his head from his paws while he said this, his blackwood staff in the crook of his arm against his shoulder.

"You did the right thing. Do not think of things in terms of black and white. In our world, a creature is what he is, though he does not necessarily need to conform to the generalities offered in books and songs and ideas about what sort of creature he is. Admiral Featherscarf is himself an undesirable, though he has never ever acted the part while I have known him. He has always been a good an honorable bird and has always been kind to me. A creature is defined by his actions, and that crow attacked our weapons master, a young squirrel, half his size, and would have thrown her over the railing and killed her if her tie off had not been secured by young Norrey Diggaburrow; and if you had not fended off her attacker and hauled her back to the deck with all of that fine strength you have been developing. You saved the life of your friend. Take solace in that."

Timmon was not sure what to say, and held his head in his paws for a few moments more, before, eyes glistening, he looked up at his old friend and said simply, "Thank you, Hoory."

Hoory made a show of acting as if checking his captain for wounds was all he had done which as medical officer was his duty and puffed out his chest and spread his wings to conceal Timmon from view somewhat, "Oh, all right then! Fearless leader! He has not a scratch on him! He fought off one of the White-Eyed Wolf's brutish henchcreatures with his bare paws and has not even a single battle wound to show for it! Some medical officer I am, he may not ever need me! He fights them off one by one and a hundred at a time and never takes a single wound. Ah, solace, I simply must be useless to such a hero after all!" With a wink and a jovial click of his beak, Hoory left the kitchen and Captain Strongtail, who remembered once more that this journey would be nothing without his friends.

At the behest of Captain Strongtail and Admiral Featherscarf, movement of the Summerswill toward the Crag slowed to a crawl. Both agreed that they needed time to facilitate a plan, time to weigh their options and more time to prepare themselves for what lay ahead.

As far as any of the creatures on the crew of the Summerswill could tell, their ship was prepared for anything; her hull had been polished to shimmering, and the iron ribcage and every nut and bolt in the iron ribcage and prow was checked over and tightened by Norrey Diggaburrow, who had no real problem being lowered over the side of the Summerswill in a sling in order to perform such tasks. Any tears in the sails, even the smallest of holes, were sewn and patched by Neesa, lest the even pinprick holes tear to larger rips in the heat of combat. The deck was swabbed, sanded, and gritted newer rougher sand so that a creature on deck might not so easily lose their footing.

All of the furniture within the Summerswill including the beds and dressers in the crews' quarters, the dining table and chairs, and every bit of furniture in the captain's cabin was secured as best as possible, whether with hempen rope, bolts, screws, or sticky pine sap.

The crew themselves were as prepared as they had ever been, and they drilled seemingly endlessly to the metronome tapping of Admiral Featherscarf's taproot walking stick.

"One, two, three, four, and counter! One, two, and attack, and one, two!" Half of the crew drilled in practice lines with whatever weapons they favored while the other half would man the rigging and the helm, waiting in tense apprehension for the appearance of another of the White-Eyed Wolf's spies or perhaps for an even more direct assault. But for almost three days on end, none came.

The Summerswill drifted lazily over the badlands east of the Crag and the Mane, waiting patiently for the enemy to make their first move as all agreed that this was perhaps the best plan of attack, to lure out the Wolf and his ship.

"When a wolf is on the hunt, he is in control of the situation. We need to draw him out into resignedly familiar territory, though different from what he is accustomed. If we had the ships or the firepower, I would suggest allocating all of our chances into following the ideal of the 'element of surprise' as it were, but we simply do not have the resources. When we control the when and where of how he maneuvers, we control the pace of the battle. What little I can tell from what stories I have heard and from those direct accounts I have from you creatures who have done battle with this evil figure before, the Sky-Skinner is a larger slower ship but has the advantage of possessing more firepower. Thus, it only seems fitting that we of the Summerswill attempt to use our speed and agility to our advantage, and we cannot manage that if we go into the crag with weapons blazing. Does that sit well with everyone present?" Hoory Softflight had proven in the last three days to be an excellent analytical thinker when it came to strategy, and the admiral and the captain were beginning to trust his thinking above all others, and so they allotted time for practice with their weapons and for outfitting the ship as best they could for battle, and the crew of the Summerswill waited.

There were few debates of strategy after that. Captain Strongtail, his first mate, Admiral Featherscarf, the captain's weapons master, Neesa Proudleap, and Mutter Stripeback, who had outfitted the Summerswill for battle all agreed with Hoory's plan of action. They simply were not many and certainly not enough to foray into the Crag alone, and their element of surprise had almost certainly been spoiled at this point by the murder that seemed to be a constant presence above the Mane, and undulating, flickering, and shifting mass of black wings and a far away echoing chorus of caws that never ceased.

So they waited. The crew of the Summerswill ate in shifts and kept a constant watch at all hours of the day. The Summerswill herself was tacked back and forth over the badlands west of the Mane. The crew practiced day in and day out with staff, sword, spear, bow, mace, and all of the heavier-mounted weapons installed by Mutter Stripeback.

It became apparent to all of the crew, little by little, the tension that their captain carried with him. It tightened in his shoulders and made his neck a taut sinewy thing, like a coiled length of hempen rope. Timmon Strongtail was growing more and more apprehensive as the days went on, thinking constantly of his family, of his quest, and of his duty to his ship. All of these weighed heavily on him, and he did not vent these thoughts in conversation with anyone over the passing days but simply internalized them, letting them build within him like a stoked furnace fire, building and building under pressure as it grew hotter and hotter. At weapon's practice he was a mute soldier; he fought with the tenacity of a seasoned veteran and worked himself to the point of near exhaustion, never saying a word. When finished, he would take his place at the helm or when forced to, eat a sparing meal of bread and water. Timmon rarely slept and when coaxed to retire to his cabin by his first mate or his medical officer, he would heed their suggestion but would never remove his manica and would simply light a candle at his desk and pore over books, often in the company of the ship's navigator, Isaac Southwinter, whom Timmon had given permission to peruse his bookshelf in the hopes of maybe finding a detailed drawing of the Crag or at the very least to replenish his store of maps which had not yet recovered from the loss they had suffered during their emergency landing in the Owl's Eye.

Isaac, present during the captain's long periods of brooding and studying, was understandably peppered with questions by both Hoory Softflight, who had a genuine concern for his captain's health and Admiral Wattle Featherscarf, who was more concerned with the mission at hand but understood that his captain's youth and inexperience might be taxing him too much. Whenever Isaac Southwinter, who spent nearly as much time as Timmon in the captain's cabin, emerged on deck whether to eat or rest in the crew's quarters, he was almost always greeted with a slue of questions:

"How did he look?"

"Is he sleeping?"

"Does the good captain appear to be suffering from exhaustion in any way, my good goose?"

"Has he read A History of the Eagles? He'll need t' read that one, lot's o' good combat details in that'n."

"Isaac, is he removing that sleeve at all? He'll develop armor sores, give him this salve at least, my good friend."

"Isaac, please."

True to his friend, Isaac Southwinter did not talk to anyone about his captain's private business. When pressed, he would pass on Hoory's salve to prevent armor sores or bring an extra cup of mulled cider or birch tea to the captain in the evening from Senna Stripeback or an extra hunk of hard bread from Brattleby Plateback. He passed on the admiral's concerns and suggested reading dutifully, but when asked about their time alone together, whether the captain had asked Isaac anything or whether they had spoken about navigational strategy during their time alone, Isaac simply clamped his bill shut and did not say a word, replying only with noncommittal honks! and nothing more.

The truth was, over the last couple of nights, Captain Strongtail and his navigator had slept almost not-at-all and, in an old tome, had discovered something that had changed all of their ideas regarding their strategy. They had pored over newly discovered maps and documents to no end, marking them over and over until their planning and replanning left many of their copies of older maps looking like veritable spider webs of movement plans and plotted scenarios.

This plan, Timmon was confident, would work. The two of them together had discovered something that would win them the war. That night, five days after the attack on Neesa Proudleap, Timmon Strongtail slept peacefully.

The next morning, Timmon Strongtail awoke refreshed and rested. He had not dreamed through the night, and though his arm was sore from wearing his sleeve for several days, sleeping in it, eating with it, reading, pacing, sitting, standing, training, steering, and working with it on, he felt reborn. The stress that had irked him these last few days had withered somewhat, now that he had formed a plan with his expert navigator. Rising from his bed, he lifted his blackwood staff from its place beside him. He had ceased to ensconce his weapon on the wall for the last few days, preferring to sleep with it beside him, lest he need it at a moment's notice. He also slept with his cutlass, a weapon he was becoming quite proficient with, resting against his nightstand unsheathed.

Timmon went to his desk and opened the top drawer, taking the bauble of salve that Hoory had passed to his through Isaac and went about applying the thick gelatinous substance to the underside of his arm, every place where the straps and belts and buckles that held the lobstered plates in place chafed against his fur and skin. He was surprised at once by the cooling effect that the substance had against his skin, and lifting it to his nose recognized the smell of mint leaf immediately. Timmon made a mental note to thank Hoory as soon as he saw him.

On his dining table was a veritable catastrophe of papers, charcoal, sextants, compasses, slide rules, and colored stones that strategists used to map ship positions. It looked as though his bookshelf and desk had voided their stomachs onto his table, and Timmon couldn't help but chuckle a little at the thought. It was the first he had laughed in as long as he could now remember.

From the back of a high-backed chair, Timmon retrieved his sword belt and bandolier, buckling them in place he sheathed his cutlass and slung his blackwood staff across his back. He once more checked all of the straps on his manica, tightening them where a few had loosened during the night and adjusted his pauldron a little higher on his shoulder so that he could easily see through the vision slit cut into it.

He ran a paw along the length of Prettle Snowhelm's feather, a habit he had developed over the last few days, something of a nervous tick at first that he realized he did without knowing while poring over documents but soon surmised that the presence of the feather should serve as a reminder of his duty and took to stroking it on purpose. It was a constant reminder of his grandfather, who had woven it into his fur shortly after he had been born among the rushes of the streams and rivers of the Valleys. The feather was a reminder of why he was here and of what he must do.

Striding like a true hero, Captain Timmon Strongtail threw open the door to his cabin and, for the first time in many days, addressed his crew as a whole:

"Meeting in the dining hall, now! All must attend! Cattatch, on the stairs, keep a wary eye on the skies! Neesa, fill him in on anything he misses!" Timmon stood there for a moment, looking at the beleaguered expressions on the faces of his crew. Brattleby was returning belowdecks with an empty pot of morning stew. Neesa and Rigger were midway up the rigging ladders, stopped in awe. Norrey had been sanding the deck and held a bucket of coarse sand in one paw, his head cocked to one side in confusion. The admiral was at the helm and was smirking slightly at his captain, pleased with this new development. Mutter had been checking the stability of the ship's railing and had stopped screwing in a bolt midturn. Senna was fawning over her son, passing him the necessary tools from a handled wooden box and had her paws full of different-sized wrenches and bolts and simply stared in disbelief at the emergence and address of Timmon Strongtail, Captain of the Summerswill. Hoory closed his eyes in a wide smile and ruffled his feathers excitedly, and Cattatch flitted down from the crow's nest for a better listen, thinking he must have heard wrong.

It was Isaac Southwinter who spurred the crew into motion; he lowered his long neck to the ground, hissing, as geese are wont to do when being aggressive, and chased and shooed every crew member on deck down the staircase to the dining hall and kitchen, his feet flapping on the deck almost comically, although there was nothing comic about an angry goose; and all the crew rolled, skidded, and stumbled down the steps in a hurry, Isaac Southwinter herding them dutifully, hissing, and honking all the while.

When the crew was all belowdeck and only Captain Timmon Strongtail and his navigator, Isaac Southwinter, remained on deck, Timmon wrapped his un-armored arm around the gooses neck in an embrace and said simply, "Thank you, my friend."

"Honk!"

The crew of the Summerswill was assembled in the dining hall; Brattleby had begun to put a meal together for the group, but Captain Strongtail had quickly put an end to that, "I want everyone's undivided attention, Brattleby. Thank you, though."

Only Cattatch Dartwing was not seated and took his position by the stairs, hopping up every few minutes to check the skies and keep a wary eye on the horizon. All others had their eyes fixed raptly on their captain, who stood at the end of the table, his first mate at his immediate right, his navigator at his left. After a minute or two of silence, Timmon spoke, jarring many of the crew from their stupor, fueled both by astonishment at the sudden transformation of their captain and their anxious apprehension at what this meeting could possibly be about, so sudden and seemingly so important. The crew was under the impression that their plan was to wait like a patient predator for the appearance of the Sky-Skinner; apparently it was not, and they eagerly awaited their captain's explanation.

"Well, I appreciate all of your cooperation with Hoory's original plan, and Hoory, I greatly value your input, and your plan was one that was obviously thoroughly thought through, but I have other ideas for this ship and this crew." There was a murmur of whispered talk among the crew.

"What does he mean?"

"Are we gonna attack?"

"He can't mean to assault the Crag?"

Timmon unslung his blackwood staff from his back in a quick motion and drove the butt end of it into the floorboards with such force that the crack it emitted silenced the entire hall.

"Sorry, all. But I want your undivided attention. If you need to speak, raise a paw or wing, and I'll address you. All right?" A slue of nodding and lightly vocalized assent ran through the crew.

"As you know I've been very distant over the last few days, and for any loss of confidence you've had in me as a captain or for any slights I've done you, be it through curt response or complete unresponsiveness, I wholeheartedly apologize. The truth is, I've been very busy with our navigator, Isaac, and I've had a lot on my mind, predominantly regarding our plan of action. Well, I do believe that our original plan of waiting for the Sky-Skinner and its crew to come to us, I do not believe we have completely lost the element of surprise. The Wolf will expect us to wait for him to make the first move, especially after we've waited this long for him to do exactly that; and that, I believe has worked in our favor, both at creating a ruse and at allowing us to have another span of time in which to prepare. All agreed?" More nods of assent followed.

"Now, Isaac, if you please." Isaac Southwinter produced from his belt a large piece of folded parchment, which he began to unfold and ease toward the center of the dining table for all to see. It was a very detailed drawing of the near regions, of the mountains of the Mane and of the Crag, but not only a structural mapping of the Crag; it was a detailed map of the construction augments to the Crag since the undesirables under the command of the White-Eyed Wolf took up residence there. Chatter ran through the crew when they began to realize what the map before them depicted, and Timmon once again struck the floorboards with his staff.

"Sorry, once again, silence please. Now if you can see this drawing, and I hope everyone can, we took this from the diary of one of the previous captain of the Summerswill. She was an otter; her name was Sierra Riverrush. During her time as captain she took very detailed notes, all of which she kept in a personal captain's log, which Isaac and I were fortunate enough to discover. In particular she kept a very detailed history of the undesirables who called the Crag their home and the renovations made after the White-Eyed Wolf took his place as their unofficial leader. It appears, from her notes, as though the Wolf himself is not only a ruthless warlord but an innovator as well. You can see from this drawing that the river at the base of the Crag flows into an inlet that siphons into another river known as the Crow's Claw, which in turn flows into a lake known as the Crow's Eye. When the Wolf took control of the Crag, he implemented a dam, I can only assume by beavers who owe their loyalty to the wolf, or perhaps by other ingenuitive creatures, that I have no way of knowing. Regardless, the dam is there, and according to Captain Riverrush, the water that cascades over the dam powers a massive waterwheel. This in turn is what commands power over their furnaces and other technologies. It's intuitive and ingenious, and although I hate to give a creature such as the Wolf any credit, what he's done is smart."

"How so?" It was Rigger who had spoken up. In his defense he had raised his hand, and Timmon did not scold him for interrupting.

"Well, he's basically tied the livelihoods of every creature in the Crag to himself. If they wish to have the kinetic power to run their machines and the other technologies that require some sort of external force, they have to follow him. He's created a political state where there was disorder before. No creature would dare disobey him while he controls their means for doing anything requiring power."

Wattle Featherscarf raised a wing.

"Yes, Admiral."

"What's the plan 'ere then?" The rest of the crew nodded along with him or turned to their captain, apprehensive, waiting to see what their answer would be.

"It's simple really. We're going to destroy the dam."

The hubbub that followed merited another strike of Timmon's blackwood staff on the floorboards. This one was much harder than he had struck previously, and the crack almost echoed in the wood-paneled dining hall.

"Quiet!" Silence followed. Mutter Stripeback raised a paw, and Cattatch flitted outside to check the skies or to escape his captain's wrath, no one was quite sure.

"Cap'n, how're we goin' to go abou' destroyin' such a dam with such a ship?"

"That's where you come in actually, Mutter."

"I do?"

"Yes. As I said before, the White-Eyed Wolf will now, I hope, be preparing to make an assault on us while we idle here, presumably waiting for him. That means his crew will be ferreting about loading cannonballs, forging weapons to replace ones that have been in disuse for some time, recaulking the hull, resanding the deck, things of that nature. According to Captain Riverrush's notes, the Sky-Skinner docks in the river at the bottom of the Crag, thereby making it all the more defensible position as any attacking ship has to navigate the canyon to get at the ship. Well, we have the advantage of being a smaller, swifter frigate. While the Wolf's creatures outfit their ship for battle, we're going to take them by surprise, and we're going to ram the Wolf's Dam." The crew of the Summerswill went wide-eyed, and many of them grew quite pale, with the sole exception of Neesa Proudleap who shot up out of her seat and punched a fist into the air almost triumphantly, although she kept her silence as Timmon had requested.

"Now I know a lot of you will think I'm mad, and I'm hoping the White-Eyed Wolf will think the same; the last thing he'll expect us to do is to attack the Crag directly, especially since our recent actions have hopefully demonstrated that's the last thing we're apt to do."

"Now Isaac has done some calculations here." Captain Strongtail signaled his navigator to produce another piece of parchment replete with so many calculations that it was quite indecipherable to all of the crew. "I assure you they're correct. Well, actually, Isaac assures me that they're correct. I don't have much of a head for numbers, Our navigator, on the other hand, is quite the arithmetic whiz. In short, they say that the best possible place for us to ram the Wolf's dam and stay aloft is directly in the center of the apex of the dam. Perfect for us in that we needn't fly deep down in the Crag where flight is most treacherous, and that we can do so quickly. Once cracked in the top of the center, the water pressure behind the dam will take care of the rest and split the dam down the middle like a paper sack filled with too much berry juice. On top of everything, hoping the Sky-Skinner is still docked, she may never be able to take off. In addition, without control over their power, the creatures of the Crag may relinquish their loyalties to the White-Eyed Wolf."

Brattleby raised an oven-mitted claw.

"Yes, Brattleby."

"What o' the Wolf's pris'ners. It's known he keeps a good many creat'rs as pris'ners. What o' them in the Crag?"

"I've addressed that, just haven't gotten around to it yet. Thank you though, Brattleby. Sierra's captain's log makes claim of a mine beneath the Mane. It's a series of deep shafts where the Wolf obtains the ores that he uses in making his weapons and technologies. She claims that is where he takes the creatures he captures, and once we've liberated the Wolf's Dam from the control of the White-Eyed Wolf, that is our next stop. Not only that, but with the way the winds have been moving, we can use the northward breeze to carry us up and out of the Crag and the few mile northeast to where the mine burrows into the Mane. We take our rescue from there. The hardest part will be circling round to ram the Wolf's Dam from west to east; that way we lose no time in continuing to the mines and, hopefully, to rescue not only my family, who I'm sure now have been taken but all the others the Wolf has taken over the years."

Neesa raised a paw and jingled the bells woven into her tail a little for attention.

"Neesa?"

She looked a little abashed to be asking, and her eyes danced left and right, slightly unsure if she should ask at all, "How do you know that the Wolf has taken your family?"

Timmon Strongtail said nothing for a few moments, and finally, eyes shut, holding back his sorrow, internalizing it; he must appear strong he told himself, he produced his blackwood staff for all to see.

The image that lazily smoked across the staff's Heart-of-Gold etchings had not changed for several days and had appeared as many days before. It was plain for all the crew to see what it was, and many of them gasped in shock at what was displayed there. In that moment, Timmon Strongtail, captain of the airship Summerswill, did shed a tear.

There, in Heart-of-Gold, was Timmon's father, his mother, and his aged grandfather behind thick iron bars and clearly deep underground, their backs straining to near breaking under sacks full to bursting with ore. Exhaustion etched their faces, and pickaxes adorned their belts. Deep under the mountains of the Mane, working to death, was Timmon Strongtail's family.

The tenacity with which the crew of the Summerswill assembled themselves after the captain had revealed the true dire straits of the situation was astounding. Within minutes, the Summerswill and her crew were armed to the teeth and prepared for war, Timmon had never seen anything like it. Admiral Wattle Feathescarf was at the helm before Timmon had even given the order, and beside him stood the ship's navigator, Isaac Southwinter, maps and diagrams in hand. Mutter was supervising the lowering of Norrey over the edge of the prow of the ship for one final check on the forward armor and ram to ensure that they were indeed prepared to destroy the Wolf's Dam, as Timmon and Isaac had planned. Neesa, Cattatch, and Rigger were high up in the rigging, checking every last grommet and knot in the sails, ensuring a swift assault and a swifter getaway. Hoory was presumably belowdeck. Over the last few days he had converted a separate dining area, off the kitchen, used only when the Summerswill was fully crewed, into a makeshift infirmary in case any of the crew was injured during the assault on the Crag. Unbeknownst to their captain, Senna and Brattleby worked hard belowdeck as well, boiling pots of oil over a raging hearth fire, preparing for battle as best two cooks could.

Timmon felt a resurgence in his heart he had not felt since first the Summerswill took flight. Their time was now, and they were prepared. They were going to take back the skies.

With a shout, Timmon Strongtail, captain of the airship Summerswill, thrust his blackwood staff forward from the prow, west over the mountains of the Mane and toward the White-Eyed Wolf and the Crag.

"Forward! Fly!"

In order to attack the Withe-Eyed Wolf's stronghold at the Crag from the west, the Summerswill and her crew had to fly due south, deeper into the badlands east of the Mane. There were no clouds here, save those formed by the rampant dust storms and twisters that scoured the lands below. What was visible beneath them was only errant rock formations that looked more like the viscous creations of nightmares than true mountains. These lands teemed with the creatures that others humbly named "undesirables." Regardless of their species, the creatures who lived this far south were dark and terrible beings, who delighted in the suffering and turmoil of others or followed chieftains and warlords who did so.

In the rare glimpses of the land beneath that Timmon managed through the wracking clouds of dust, he could see small tribal villages, replete with fluttering banners and huts that looked as though, Timmon feared, they were made of tempered hides. Of skins. The creatures who witnessed the passing of the Summerswill overhead left their tents and houses and huts with their necks craned to the sky, followed immediately by calls to arms. These creatures would disappear into their dwellings for a moment, only to reemerge armed to the teeth with blades and axes and shields bearing crude insignia. They clashed their weapons against their armor creating an awful din that could be heard only faintly as high as the Summerswill flew. It was not until the militias of undesirables broke out their war horns that the noise they created truly reached the crew of the Summerswill.

Har-OOOOO! Har-OOOOOO! Har-OOOOOOO!

"The tribes be assemblin', it seems." Wattle Featherscarf remarked to his captain while he maintained their course south at the helm.

"Why, though?"

"We're clearly not the Sky-Skinner, lad. They know there's other creatures in the skies again. N' the majority o' them owe their loyalty to the Wolf." The admiral tossed his great floppy hat out of his eyes with a flick of his wrinkled neck, "If'n we succeed in this mission here, lad, the repercussions will last a long time"

"Repercussions?"

"If'n we kill the Wolf, the creatures o' the Badlands will be in disarray. They may turn on one another, or they may turn north. Remains t' be seen I think."

Timmon thought on this a moment, clutching his blackwood staff close against his shoulder with his arm clothed in iron before he said, "We're doing the right thing, aren't we, Admiral?"

"The right thin'? Well, lad, it may not be the right thin' in totality, but it's the only thin' to do. If'n we want the skies to be free, and every creature aboard this ship does, then we have to kill the Wolf." He turned and stared a moment into Timmon with his ice-blue eyes, seemingly boring a hole through him, as his stare was wont to do.

"And then? What about after we've done what we came here to do?"

"There be no more eagles, lad. They left this land for the lifting o' warmer winds. After this, it'll be up to us to keep the skies free. You'd better be n' this for the long hall young'n." Wattle Featherscarf smiled at Timmon Strongtail then, the lines around his beak and eyes wrinkling his face until it looked like naught but a smear of puddled skin.

"I hadn't realized." Captain Strongtail stole another glance over the railing of the Summerswill at the teeming masses below, their warhorns bellowing out the call to arms.

"Our actions have consequences, lad. Face 'em, or stay home."

"This is my home now."

"Good lad. Almos' there now, we'll turn to the west, then north, and then to the Crag, we'll finish what you started."

"You talk about this like it's a game, Admiral. Like we might as well be playing cards. How are you so cavalier right now?"

"Lad, you take thin's in life too seriously, n' you lose all your perspective. Even the serious thin's. Live it all n' the now, n' live like there ain't no tomorrow, take the helm, I'm hungry." The admiral let the helm go, and the Summerswill lurched to port for a moment, moving with the winds that steered her sails, and Timmon felt their entire deck sway beneath him before he lunged for the helm and wrenched the rudder back on course with all the strength he could muster at an instant's notice.

"You're hungry!"

"Can' go to battle on an empty stomach, lad!"

By that evening, the Summerswill had turned west, and Admiral Wattle Featherscarf, after a hearty meal of boiled potatoes, hard bread baked with butter and garlic, and sugar-covered blueberries, was back at the helm. Timmon Strongtail had retired for the night to the captain's cabin and had invited Hoory Softflight to join him for tea. Timmon, though anxious, was hard-pressed to pass up a pot of Senna Stripeback's chamomile tea and sipped lightly at a cup, sitting across from Hoory. Both of them occupied a pair of high-backed black oak chairs; between them was a map of the badlands and the southern regions of Sylva which Timmon had been studying. Timmon had removed his manica at Hoory's behest, and a bandage soaked in the soothing salve that Hoory had prescribed now wrapped his arm, cooling Timmon's stressed muscles and the chafing wounds that had began to develop from the prolonged wear of his armor. Monocle in place, Hoory finally asked what had been on his mind for some minutes.

"Captain, why have you invited me to your quarters this evening, though it joys me to see you finally remove that beastly armor, and I am quite enamored with this tea, I would be remiss if I did not allow that I sensed something else was afoot." He sipped at his tea, looking at Timmon Strongtail from under his heavily lidded eyes.

"There is, Hoory. I need you to tell me something, and I would like the truth."

"Oh, oh, oh, of course! I would not dream of falsifying evidence to you my courageous captain. What can I help you with?"

"I want to know about the White-Eyed Wolf. You've been around this world; you've heard the stories, and you, above all others, I value as a creature who can separate fact from fiction. If I'm going to do this right, I want to know my enemy." Timmon put on the sternest, most captainlike face he could muster, which was difficult to manage with a porcelain teacup in his paw.

"You have been reading Sienna Riverrush's journal, have you not? She was a wise captain if the tales are true; and it is true, one must know one's enemy if one is to triumph over an adversary." Hoory sipped at his tea for a moment, collecting his thoughts, "Here is what I know, both from stories and from hearsay . . .

"A long time ago, there was a pack of wolves, the largest pack that the Valleys or the badlands, all of Sylva itself had ever seen. This pack was ruled over a ruthless alpha male, who ruled over his wolves with an iron paw and a strict regime. Time went on, and little by little, this alpha male took control of nearly every pack in the world until every wolf owed his allegiance to this alpha male. He was a deity among his kind."

"In this same pack, as is with every pack of wolves, where there is an alpha, there is an omega. This wolf was the very lowest of the low. He was trod on by every member of this innumerable pack, and nothing he ever did would see him rise in the hierarchy of this regime. One day, hoping to assert himself as a true member of the pack, this omega wolf challenged his alpha. They say that the fight that ensued was over in seconds, and the omega wolf was defeated. Beaten, bloodied, and disgraced ever further, this wolf left the pack. He traveled farther and farther away until he had reached the ends of the world, high in the north where the lands are always winter. Here he could find no food, he could find no shelter, he found nothing but a desolate wasteland of white."

"Here he remained for some time until a creature of a different sort set upon him. They say a great arctic bear, larger than anything known anywhere south of the lands where winter never thaws, set upon him. This beast was ferocious, without pity, and hungry. These two creatures, the arctic bear, and the disgraced omega wolf did battle for their lives. It's said that they duel continued for days and days. At one moment, a horrible swipe of this arctic bear's paw took the omega wolf's eye. But in the end, the wolf defeated the bear, and in celebration of his victory, he feasted on his defeated enemy and took his skin for his own."

"That is how this wolf, this White-Eyed omega wolf returned to his pack. He wore the skin of a great arctic bear for a cloak, and his single eye now shone with the icy cold fury of the lands where winter never thaws."

Timmon was rapt, "What happened to this pack, Hoory."

"The White-Eyed Wolf killed them. They sent him away in disgrace; they trod on him and forced him to the back-end of every meal and every hunt and every instance of every day of his entire life, and when he returned, he slew every one of them. That, Captain, is what you face."

By dawn the next day, the Summerswill and her crew were deep in the Badlands and heading west to loop around behind the Crag and surprise the forces of the White-Eyed Wolf. At this point, every nut and bolt in the hull, every cannon and every grommet in the sails had been checked over half-a-dozen times. Spirits were determined and lost in solemn preparation for the battle to come, but outlooks were high.

Timmon Strongtail was at the helm; Brattleby and the admiral were at his side. Brattleby was clad in his iron spaulders and gorget, and the admiral had donned a breastplate that was far too large for him and hung around his wrinkled neck like a poorly tailored iron shirt. All three wore their weapons, Brattleby his mace, the admiral his taproot walking stick and a wickedly curved dagger at his side, and Timmon's cutlass hung off of his belt loop; his blackwood staff was nestled in the crook of his shoulder as he steered the ship.

A moment later, Isaac Southwinter strode up the steps to the helm, his tricornered hat cocked sideways on his head. His belt was stuffed like an overflowing cornucopia with papers, maps, compasses, pencils, sextants, slide rules, and a long thin rapier with a basket hilt. He wore only a leather jerkin, studded with iron over his breast for armor, his loup danced gaily on its chain about his neck as he wobbled up the steps.

"We're nearing our turning point, Cap'n. Honk! A few more minutes at this speed, and we'll need to turn north."

"All right, Isaac. Thank you. Is everyone's tie off secured? I want to be ready."

"I'll check with Neesa, Cap'n, though I'm sure they are." The ship's navigator turned on his webbed feet and waddled back down the stairs to root out the ship's weapons master.

"Best not be too apprehensive, lad. The ship's been checked over a dozen times by now. Makes the crew nervous if'n you're nervous. Jus' steer an' look the part. Let your feelin's be too known n' they'll spread to the crew, always remember that." Wattle Featherscarf shook his hat back from his eyes, looking forward into the buff and fawn clouds swirling in front of them and beneath them. The sounds of the war horns had died down as the Summerswill had ascended higher into the sky so as not to be so easily spotted, lest the undesirables below made their movements known to those in the Crag.

"Thank you, Admiral. I'll keep that in mind." Timmon absentmindedly tacked the Summerswill forward a little, pressing down on their speed pedal the slightest bit as he heard the call from below,

"Winds be shifting north by three knots, Cap'n. We're in the lee of the Crag now, steer us north, and we'll be in place. Honk!"

Timmon did just that, spinning the ship's wheel starboard, savoring the feeling of the deck yawning beneath his feet and the bulk of the frigate lurching gently, her propeller gaining speed as he put just a little more weight onto her acceleration pedal.

"Thank you, Isaac! Let's go crew. Brattleby, check with everyone belowdeck and in the rigging, I want all creatures aboard on alert. Check with Hoory in the infirmary as well; assure he's prepared for anything."

"Aye, Cap'n. I'll make it so." Brattleby lumbered down the helm steps, armor clanking. Timmon noticed that the great-tattooed tortoise still had not removed his apron or oven mitts, as though on the eve of battle, the ship's chef extraordinaire was still prepared to whip up a pot of leek and lentil stew, and the captain of the Summerswill chuckled a little at this.

"Good, lad. Laugh. A light heart is one at ease." The admiral smirked as well, placing a wing on Timmon's iron-lobstered arm.

His mind a little lighter, Timmon granted himself a moment's reprieve from his worries, letting the tension in his shoulders leak away like rainfall. He shut his eyes, and he relished the feeling of the wind on his face and the gentle pull of the breeze through Prettle Snowhelm's feather.

In that moment of solace, the first crows of the White-Eyed Wolf's murder slammed into the deck of the Summerswill.

In half a heartbeat chaos erupted on the deck. A dozen crows, perhaps a score, had crashed into the Summerswill, their bodies a flurry of dark wings and sharp beaks, their necks and legs adorned with trinkets and bangles of a thousand-brilliant colors. Many of them wore iron spurs on their shanks, and many more still had filed their toenails and beaks to wicked points. They cawed and screamed in the most haunting and horrible cacophony of noise that Timmon had ever heard. In that moment the admiral wrenched the helm from his grasp and shouted at his captain, "Go, lad! Do what you were born to do!" With a great wrench of the helm, the admiral drove the Summerswill to port, slanting the deck in the hopes that some of the crows may lose their footing before it was gained. Timmon Strongtail clung to the railing with one paw and readied his blackwood staff with his other, his eyes narrowing, and his shoulders bunching with tension as he waited for the moment when the admiral would right the deck once more; and the instant that moment came, Timmon vaulted over the railing to the deck below and into the fray.

He saw before him the tumult of battle. His crew had sprang into action, and all were actively in combat with their dark adversaries already. Those crows that had lost their footing were in scrambles trying to stand, and one was quickly dispatched by Neesa, rapier in hand and quick to strike as any viper. Brattleby Plateback did not flinch from the battle in front of him as a trio of crows lashed out with their spurs and their sharpened beaks at his armored shell but focused instead on driving back the half-dozen in front of him with great labored swings of his mace. He had tucked his head and feet deep into his shell, such that little of him was available to counter-blows from his enemies, and he drove many of them to the edges of the deck where they were forced to either take wing or be smashed against the railing.

Cattatch and Hoory were locked in furious battle above the deck, swirling in and out of the rigging and sails that they knew so well, catching their opponents unaware and trapping them in the Summerswill's rope ladders and luring them into collisions with the ship's masts.

Back to back, mother and son, Senna and Mutter Stripeback danced across the deck in tight circles, striking out with their enormous paws, dealing blow after blow to any unwary enough to draw near, the fire of battle flamed in both of their eyes as it had many years before.

Rigger Diptail was making quite a show of spinning his cutlass skillfully, though seemed unsure of whether to engage any crows directly until one set upon him from his side and knocked him to the deck, beating at his face with its great black wings. It only stopped when its head was separated from its body, a swift cut from Isaac Southwinter's blade was the catalyst.

Beside the helm, Norrey fought off any crows smart enough to assault the admiral, who focused only on steering the ship, and as battle-hardened as he was, an onlooker might not even notice that the admiral was in the midst of a melee, he was quite calm.

Blackwood staff in paw, Timmon Strongtail launched himself at the first crow to notice him, a thick-breasted creature whose eyes he could not discern from the darkness of its body. It wore a hundred necklaces of as many colors, and its beak was tipped in an iron point, filed to an end that glimmered like a razor. The great bird lunged at Timmon, spreading its wings and rushing straight on, flapping and scuffling along the deck. Timmon sidestepped this attack quickly and lashed out at the birds head as he spun about, solidly connecting with the undesirable's skull. As the bird fell to the deck, Timmon lashed out with another pair of blows, the first to the birds nearest wing, the snap of bone assuring him that he had broken its bone, the second to the small of the birds back, which knocked the wind from the creature and left it gasping on the deck.

Quickly readying for another bout, Timmon whirled to find Isaac Southwinter across the deck, his back against the railing, being assaulted by a pair of black birds. Timmon sprinted and closed the distance between them in a few long strides and, when close, brought his manica across his chest and tackled the first crow to the deck, its head connected with the stone-hard wood and an instant later also connected with the interlocking iron joints of Timmon's sleeve as he struck the bird with the backside of his arm.

The second crow swung around to attack this new foe, when a moment later, Isaac's blade emerged from the center of its breast, and the crow fell to the deck to reveal the ship's navigator standing behind it, blade in wing.

"The Crag, Cap'n! It's beneath us! Honk!"

Timmon looked out over the railing in time to feel the Summerswill begin to dip at her prow as Admiral Wattle Featherscarf made a beeline for the Wolf's Dam beneath them, and there beneath the ship, far, far below, was the emerging outline of the canyon known to all of Sylva as the Crag.

In that same moment, the sound of war horns became clear again, and Timmon bore witness to the cloud of crows that spewed forth from the Crag like hornets from a nest.

Moments became seconds and seconds counted themselves until they nearly numbered a minute, but Timmon's world moved in slow motion as the Summerswill approached the Wolf's Dam, streaming downward as fast as she could, her bowsprit wreathed in iron and shining like a honed blade. All around him the chaos of the battle on the deck roared like a blazing fire as his crew fought off what remained of the White-Eyed Wolf's murder, though a thousand more streamed outward from the Crag like flies disturbed from a feast, tumbling and screaming higher and higher into the air betwixt the ship and the dam, blocking the way. Then a sound broke through everything, low at first, then haunting and bellowed like a cry from the belly of the most fearsome creature of Timmon's worst dreams. Through the whistle of the wind, the screams of the crows on deck and before them, through the clash of iron on iron and the creaking strain of the sails taut to tearing with speed, a howl rose from the Crag.

"Howw-OOOOOOOOO-A-ROOOOOOOOOOWWW!"

Surrounded by friend and foe alike all engaged in furious combat, Timmon felt for that moment that he was truly alone in the world as the howl of the White-Eyed Wolf leaked like ire from a wound from the Crag below, echoing a dozen times through the canyon and spreading like a poisoned mist through the air. Timmon felt it slither into his bones and deep into his chest where his heart beat and flooded his every vein with the chill that frosted spiral patterns through his body.

As they grew closer, Timmon watched as his eyes adjusted through the dust storms and the spray of water from the Crow's Eye below as the Summerswill dipped lower and lower. From within the Crag emerged the first hints of the stronghold that the Wolf had spent his years building. Watchtowers and long houses of timbered logs clung to the walls of the crag like cobwebs to the structure of an abandoned home. Steam and smoke rose from the depths of the canyon where the fires of the forges and furnaces never ceased their burning and the blooded glow from them underlit every facade of the Wolf's fortress like an ancient telling scary stories from beside a campfire. Every inch of the Crag was bannered in red and black and tapestries that depicted a single iris drawn and painted and etched in the purest white that the undesirables of the Crag could muster. Every surface was as a nightmare, a haunted place where every wall and cliff face, and dark corner was full of sleepless omniscient eyes, always watching.

As the captain of the Summerswill took all of this in, the crows of the murder launched themselves forward, a writing, spinning black mass of ebony feathers and honed beaks and iron-spiked shanks that screamed a cacophony war song of caws that drowned out all else.

"Cannons! Hand cannons all!" Mutter Stripeback had stolen below for only a few moments time, but his deep bellowing cut through the sights that had transfixed his captain. In his muscled arms was a bundle of hand cannons preloaded with bola cartridges, and these he passed out to every crew member within reach.

"Fire into the murder! We have to reach the dam!" Timmon shouted, his trance broken, his heart raced with the pace of their mission, and he ripped a hand cannon from Mutter's arms, bracing the butt of the gun against his shoulder as Mutter had shown him and sighting down the barrel. There a tiny piece of straw had been anchored to help gauge the movement of the wind when firing, an instant after trying to level the barrel the straw broke off and flew past Timmon Strongtail's ear, the Summerswill was racing. The crows racing toward him, Timmon stood toward the prow, a number of crew beside him though he did not look to see who they were, only sighted his hand cannon and shouted, "Fire!"

Smoke and fire erupted from the barrels of the guns, and a volley of iron bolas shot forward into the approaching murder where a score of crows were caught tangled in the iron-laced ropes and snagging iron balls. Their wings caught, and their balance frayed a number of them tumbled head over claw to the soil below, spiraling down and down like fluttering petals off of a dark flower. Still, more came, and the crew of the Summerswill reloaded their guns. Timmon saw now, Neesa, Norrey, Cattatch, Mutter, and Senna beside him in a firing line, while the rest of his crew carried on the first behind them, clearing the deck of the few crows who still fought on.

Cartridges in place and their flintlocks cocked back, the firing line again raised their hand cannons to their shoulders, apprehensive and squeezed their triggers in another volley of flames and iron when their captain shouted, "Fire!"

More crows caught their wings and legs and beaks in the flurry of iron and thick ropes, catching to one another and fighting to stay aloft, failing they fell in droves.

A shout called from the helm, the admiral's gravelly voice reached the prow of the ship, "Brace for impact!"

Timmon saw then how low they flew over the Crow's Eye below them, and the first hints of waves from the fish-fin sail on the belly of the Summerswill, a storm of green-brown water spraying up all around them. Rushing toward them was the Wolf's Dam, a great timber wall covered in red flags, and the Summerswill sped toward it, ironclad bowsprit aimed squarely at its center.

Lower and lower the Sumerswill sank until her belly fin and port and starboard wings dipped low into the waters of the Crow's Eye raised great waves at the ship's sides. Walls of brown-green water rose up beneath them, and a deluge crashed over the dam in a torrent. Timmon Strongtail sprang to his left and grabbed the deck railing, clinging with all of his might as did the rest of his crew. An instant later the impact that wracked the ship drove every deck-bound creature into the air. Cattatch and Hoory rose into the air, flapping their wings wildly to keep pace with the ship. A hail of splinters and broken timbers flew into the air and, for a brief instant, filled the sky with spinning black shards of wood. The crows of the murder who remained between the Summerswill and the dam were gone, driven beneath the water as they tumbled beneath the belly of the ship or cast spiraling into the sky as they rattled off the iron-clad bowsprit, wings bent and broken and crooked. The Wolf's Dam split down the center with a crack that resounded through the Crag like a thunderclap, and beneath the gap that the Summerswill punched through the apex of the dam, a million tiny springs of water fountained outward under the pressure of the Crow's Eye.

"WOOO-HOOO!" Admiral Wattle Featherscarf whooped in glee as the stern of the Summerswill cleared the end of the dam, her great rear propeller cutting into the rushing waterfall it had left behind for a second before the ship rolled out over the Crag.

Once past the threshold of the dam, the thousand fountains burst. Tiny cracks in the timber wall of dam split open one by one, from tiny rivulets of water into great geysers, and finally into a cascading wall of water, bursting at the seams like an overfilled sack. A drumroll of cracks and snaps and creaks of splintering wood chorused through the Crag as the flood spilled into the canyon beneath the Summerswill.

The cobweb buildings clinging to the walls of the canyon began to lose their hold, and the smallest of them were torn from their bindings by the tide. Sodden banners were ripped free, and below the crew of the Summerswill, the shapes of a thousand undesirable creatures skittered this way and that, desperate to avoid the onrushing water. Those who could clung to sturdy beams, those who could take wing beat their soaked feathers against the rising cloud of steam from the furnace fires below; and those who were unfortunate were swept away beneath the water, down the canyon.

Timmon saw all of this as something gripped his heart with long icy fingers and tensed every muscle in his body. Something not unlike guilt took him as he watched his enemies flow away beneath him. On every side of him his crew erupted into celebration as the admiral brought the Summerswill back up above the Crag, higher into the air. Cheers and calls of celebration echoed around the deck and through the spray of water and rising clouds of steam from below, but Timmon felt hollow and weak, like a guttered candle or an empty scabbard. He turned on his heel, blackwood staff in one hand, hand cannon in another, his cutlass still sheathed at his side, and stared beyond him at his crew, all dancing merrily and leaping into the air in exuberance.

"They never saw us comin'!"

"We did it!"

"We've won!"

"Three cheers for Cap'n Strongtail!"

"Hip! Hip! Hooray!"

"NO!" Timmon shouted as loud as he could and threw his gun to the deck with a furious arc of his iron-sleeved arm. His crew stopped midmotion; all eyes were on their captain, whose shoulders shook with the very effort of trying to slow his breathing and his heart which beat thickly against his ribcage. "We just slew many, we will not celebrate that. What we did was only necessary. The Wolf is defeated, as are his minions, but we will never, never celebrate death while aboard my ship. Is that understood?" As if on cue, rain began to fall as the Summerswill ascended higher and higher toward the darkening clouds above them. It began with a sprinkling of cold water and turned quickly to a deluge of sheets of whipping water that slapped the deck with a fury that was echoed only in the fire behind Timmon Strongtail's eyes.

The shoulders of every member of his crew slumped a little, heavy with the weight of their embarrassment, of their guilt, of their shame. One by one, without being ordered so, the crew of the Summerswill went about their duties, checking their tie offs, manning the rigging and taking inventory of their weapons, checking the deck for damage, and tending what minor wounds they had suffered. Only Hoory Softflight remained behind, and he stood in front of his captain for some time without uttering a word. Timmon stared at the deck beneath his feet, trying desperately to occupy his mind with memorizing the pattern of the knots and whorls in the wood rather than meet the eyes of his old friend. When he finally did look up several minutes later, Timmon met Hoory's knowing, golden eyes. He had removed his monocle, and tears stood openly streaming down the feathers of his cheeks; he steeped to his captain and took him in a feathery embrace that Timmon eagerly returned, not caring whether or not they were seen by his crew, not caring whether they witnessed a show of emotion or sadness from their captain, caring only that all of his friends were still alive and well and that he was not alone in his quest.

"You're absolutely on the side of right in this, my captain. You have demonstrated more than I ever believed you could, and you did so with honor. I am wholly proud of you."

"Thank you, Hoory." Timmon let his friend go, though Hoory did not break the embrace for several more seconds.

The Summerswill turned north toward the mines where the White-Eyed Wolf kept his prisoners, locked away in work camps deep beneath the surface, harvesting ore for his forges and all of his schemes. Timmon Strongtail and his crew believed that their adventure was over, that the undesirables of the Wolf had been defeated, and that the Wolf himself was deep beneath the waters of the Crow's Eye at the bottom of the Crag.

None of them had noticed the dark shape that now followed them north like a blemish in the sky where the sun had always neglected to shine, and through the rain the two ships strove north.

It was a several hour flight to the Mane, and the mines of the White-Eyed Wolf. The mood on the airship Summerswill was somber. Since the attack on the Wolf's Dam at the Crag, they had not been harassed. No crows had pestered them, no undesirables blew their war horns beneath them, and aside from the driving rain, the flight seemed to be quite uneventful.

No one spoke. The crew, one by one visited Hoory's infirmary belowdeck. No member of the crew was seriously injured, but many had smaller cuts and bruises that Hoory insisted on tending to.

Timmon Strongtail stood at the helm beside the admiral who still steered the ship. Despite his slick fur, Timmon was quite cold and had donned a long cloak to keep out the chill of the rain, his hood covered his head; and he had tucked Prettle Snowhelm's feather down his collar, his blackwood staff rested against his shoulder.

"We did the righ' thing, lad."

"Did we though?" Timmon was still unsure.

"Aye. Though I'd be surprised if'n we saw the last o' the Wolf."

"Beg your pardon?" Timmon's eyes widened, and he turned to face his first mate, "What do you mean?"

"I mean his like don' pack up n' leave so easily. Doubt if that little spill will deter him too much."

"I see." Timmon was all of the sudden a quiver with thought.

"We got a lot o' work ahead o' us, Cap'n. As I said before, this ain't over." The admiral steered north, the rain running in rivers down his floppy hat.

"As you say." Timmon turned and looked out over the stern of the ship, back toward the Crag. It was then that he noticed what followed them.

A great black shape stalked behind them, massive sails like ebon eyelids, tattered and frayed like the wings of a crippled bird. Its hull was a skeletal hulk of mismatched shades of gray and black metal; its prow adorned with a massive white circle painted with a pupil of deepest onyx. It was not unlike the form of a massive, rotting barracuda, skulking behind the Summerswill, eagerly following its prey. Aboard the deck a thicket of creatures armed to the teeth with all manner of blades and maces and poorly wrought weapons swayed back and forth, eager for their first taste of battle in many years. Atop the helm stood a single figure, tall and slender with thick broad shoulders. A pair of long tattered ears topped its head; a silver-white cloak draped its back, and a single ivory eye stared out from its misshapen dark form, glittering and horrible. From far away, Timmon caught the yellow glint of a smile curling across its face.

Timmon saw the Wolf for the first time, and for the second time that day heard his howl.

"Howw-OOOOOOOOO-A-ROOOOOOOOOOWWW!"

Timmon Strongtail, captain of the airship Summerswill, stood struck with fear for more than a moment. The howl that split the sky and pierced the rain like a lightning bolt froze him. His veins seemed to fill with ice, and his heart palpated in ripples of off-sync beats; Timmon's stomach turned over, and he tasted bile in the back of his throat. Through the surging rain he could plainly make out the darker figure of the Sky-Skinner against the almost jet-black clouds. It was a hunched and monstrous thing like a crushed beetle that had only just began to reform its own exoskeleton, albeit with a menagerie of crudely cut metal and taut-pulled canvasses that Timmon was sure in his heart were actually haphazardly woven skins. Its main mast was a crooked spike with rigging like black spiderwebs. It was more like the finger of something long dead clawing its way up from the soil than the mast of a true frigate. The sails of the Sky-Skinner were blacker than midnight, replete with a million holes of every size and patched a thousand times with cloth that only seemed darker than the adjacent patches. Each sail, for there were many, bore the insignia of the Wolf, a massive white iris, centered with a perfect black pupil that was not simply black but seemed to be painted with the complete absence of color. The entirety of the ship was not a sight in itself but rather the experience of being terrified. In truth, it was at least three times the size of the Summerswill, and Timmon Strongtail felt the hope drain from his chest through his paws and the tip of his tail, slipping away as easily as rain poured from the wrinkles in his cloak.

It was Admiral Wattle Featherscarf who called out the first orders, "You lot! Arm yourselves! Mutter, Brattleby, Rigger, t' the gun deck! ON THE DOUBLE! Chop, chop, creatures! Hoory, belowdeck! Cattatch get y'self t' the crow's nest fast as y' like, PLEASE!" Still holding the helm, he buffeted Timmon in the face with one wing and caught his eyes, flipping his sodden hat out of his eyes and stared down his captain, "Lad, y' better get hold o' y'self right quick. We got ourselves a battle comin' like none y' ever seen. Captain, orders?"

As quickly as he had felt everything drain out of him, Timmon Strongtail snapped back into himself like a fired crossbow, shoulders tensed, blackwood staff clenched tight in his paw, he shirked his cloak from his back in one fleet motion and flicked his head back to free his sodden eagle feather from where it had stuck to the fur of his neck. Prettle Snowhelm's ivory feather streaming out behind him in the gusts of wind and torrents of falling rain like a banner of heraldry, Timmon struck his blackwood staff on the deck at a fast rhythm, setting the pace for his crew.

"Move, move, move! We will not lose this day! This is our time, my friends! We take it or we die trying!" He turned to his first mate, the admiral next to him, and said to him only, "Bring the Summerswill about, open up our guns on the port side.

I'll give the volley order; once all our barrels are empty, take us back and speed toward the Skinner as fast as we can manage."

"Y' mean to ram them, lad?"

"No, take us past them, our starboard to their starboard, I want to empty our other guns into them point blank."

"Y' think that's a good idea, Cap'n?"

"We're faster than them; we can come upon them, unload, and be past them before they know what to expect." Timmon Strongtail was resolute, his face set and unyielding.

"As you wish, Cap'n." Wattle ripped the ship's wheel to the right, and the Summerswill began to come about, gliding almost effortlessly despite the howling wind and rain, bearing her port side to the oncoming Sky-Skinner.

A deafening series of booms cut into the night sky. Eruptions of orange and yellow and red curdled out from beneath the bowsprit of the Sky-Skinner, and a narrow whistle shrieked past Timmon Strongtail's ear, its tailwind pulling at the eagle feather woven into his fur.

"They have for'ard guns, Cap'n!" Wattle's eyes were wide and cold, a mixed display of surprise and discipline-suppressed rage.

"Answer them!" Timmon yelled his command, his ears still ringing from the cannonball that had narrowly missed striking him. No sound of torn sail or cracked timber had resounded following the fired shots, and Timmon took that to mean that they had been missed by the first volley of fire from the Sky-Skinner, and he was not prepared to think that his ship or his crew would be so lucky a second time.

As he counted the seconds while the Sky-Skinner's crew presumably reloaded their cannons, Timmon could feel the pressure of anticipation build within him, when at last, after only a short time but what had seemed like an eternity, their port side was open to fire, he shouted his command so loud that he nearly lost his voice.

"Fire!"

The concussions of the Summerswill's cannons were heard much closer but felt more than taken by ear. The deck beneath Captain Strongtail reverberated and shook. The vibrations rattled up Timmon's feet and his blackwood staff and finally to his ribcage where he felt almost as if the breath he drew in that instant was one of gunpowder and iron.

The cannonballs moved too quickly to be seen, but they left behind trails of exploded raindrops, evaporated by the steam off of the iron balls such that trace trails of gray spirited through the darkness toward the Sky-Skinner; and Timmon Strongtail was rewarded with the sound of splintering wood and the cries of the White-Eyed Wolf's crew as pinprick explosions sparked along the Sky-Skinner's hull.

A fire lit up in Timmon's eyes, something that had been there all along like dying coals that had finally been stoked to life, the battle had been joined.

Rain whipped against the deck, kicking up a constant mist of broken droplets along the entirety of the deck and hull of the Summerswill, and as the ship turned back to face the Sky-Skinner head-on and catapulted forward under the guidance of the admiral, the first staccato spikes of lightning began to split the sky. Deep, growling thunder boomed off in the distance beyond notice at first, then closer as the minutes passed in the first airship engagement since the last stand. Finally, as Timmon Strongtail, fluttering white feather whipping out behind him, lobstered iron arm resplendent and slick with rain water, and eyes afire with the dithyrambic experience of midair strife, the first white-hot veins of electricity began to crackle and explode all around the twin ships.

The crew of the Summerswill was a flurry of movement, of purpose. They scurried about the ship, checking the sail's attachments and the tie offs. Belowdeck, Brattleby and Mutter reloaded the cannons, stocking the barrel with gunpowder, and loading each with a stout iron ball.

As the Summerswill shot forward toward her opponent, the Sky-Skinner, a second volley of cannon shot erupted from the prow of the enemy ship from just beneath the bowsprit. Iron tore through the night sky, glistening trails of rain marking the paths of the artillery. Many of the cannonballs missed their intended target except one. A single cannonball struck the Summerswill's ironclad prow, tearing a divot in the plates of armor and spinning upward. Much of its velocity lost tearing into metal, the cannonball rotated above the ship for a moment before crashing down into the deck with a thud and rolling toward the railing as the Summerswill flew on. It fell through a water outlet gap in the ship's railing, down into the blackness of the sky beneath the two ships.

Through it all, Timmon's breath had caught in his throat. He had not thought they would be lucky enough to be missed by a volley from the Sky-Skinner a second time, and he had been quite correct. Now he only hoped that they would be lucky enough to take the brunt of the firepower from the enemy in the prow where Mutter's armoring had just proven to have been an excellent addition to the Summerswill.

"Forward! Fly!" Timmon Strongtail had made his presence known on the deck of the Summerswill, waving his blackwood staff high above his head, the shaft of his grandfather's gift now gleaming and radiating like the rays of the sun in the darkness of the night and the clouding fall of the rain. Beneath his feet, the deck lurched forward, and Timmon felt his balance shift backward with the speed at which they moved; balancing himself with his tail, he ran forward, stopping short of the prow and shouting as he had heard his grandfather tell that creatures in battle often did. He had told Timmon stories of creatures who would cry the names of their homes, the loved ones, and their pride in the heat of battle, their war cries being true to their hearts. Timmon did not think; he did not consider what his battle call would be; it was the cry that found him . . .

"Summerswill!"

From behind him the call caught breath in the voices of the rest of his crew. Cattatch fluttered back and forth about the crow's nest calling, "Summerswill, Summerswill, Summerswill!"

Belowdeck the heady rough voices of Brattleby and Mutter and Senna vibrated under Timmon's feet, "Summerswill!"

Neesa, Norrey, and Rigger, manning the harpoon guns and in the rigging chorused together, "Summerswill, Summerswill, Summerswill!"

In his infirmary, Hoory heard the cries from above and hooted to himself, his eyes squinting with pride, "Summerswill!"

At the helm, clawed foot pressed firmly against the acceleration pedal, floppy hat askew, steering the subject of the battle cries toward her enemy, Admiral Wattle Featherscarf grated under his breath, a bare whisper, but one full of knowing and plume, "Summerswill."

Racing toward their enemy, the crew of the Summerswill barely heard the answering call above their own exclamations, though the crew of the Sky-Skinner was wholly aware of their captain's own battle call; and through respect, admiration, and above all, fear, they soldiered on under his white-eyed banner, trekking closer to engaged combat with their enemies aboard the Summerswill. His call was haunting, lilting, and hushed rising to a stentorian air.

"Howw-OOOOOOOOO-A-ROOOOOOOOOOWWW!"

Careening through the sky, the Summerswill and her crew struck onward toward the Sky-Skinner with a fervor born of an embattled mindset and a renewed sense of honor. Belowdeck, the cannons had been reloaded with shells and cannonballs, Mutter, Senna, and Brattleby ready at a moment's notice to ignite their fuses and fire a volley of flame, iron, and sail-rending shrapnel.

From the helm, Captain Strongtail called out to his crew on the deck, "Neesa, Norrey, Rigger, Cattatch, man the harpoon guns, be prepared to fire straight into their deck, and then cut the lines!" With an ardent swiftness, the four took to the mounted harpoon guns on the ship's starboard side, swinging their harpoon guns into position over the edge of the deck and sighting down the barrels, awaiting the moment when the Sky-Skinner would be within range.

"Onward, Admiral, bring us right close." Timmon was like a stonewall, eyes fixed on his enemy, and every muscle from his neck to the tip of his tail tensed with eager anticipation.

"We're closin' fast, Cap'n!"

"Bring us to her starboard, we're going in."

Wind and rain that hit the deck like iron hail rushed over the Summerswill as the ship closed in on her enemy. Timmon Strongtail gripped his blackwood staff so tightly that his paw began to cramp with veins of heat; he did not blink despite the wind coursing over his eyes; he was set on his target as so many airship captains had been since times before memory could serve. They came nearer and nearer, in one minute, perhaps two, they would be within range of the harpoons. His resolve burned inside him like smoldering coals, fanned into spouting tiny bites of flame and white-hot dancing embers.

Moments slipped by like swirling flakes of snow, one by one and a thousand at a time. The world spun by Timmon in a flurried blur of motion, fixed around the central point of the approaching and nearer-growing Sky-Skinner.

It seemed at the same time to Timmon as though a thousand years had passed and, like an instant, had barely begun to go by when the Sky-Skinner broke the threshold of the Summerswill, the massive ship to the starboard of its smaller opponent. The pair were like a fly attacking a songbird, a horribly disfigured and gaunt songbird like a black swallow spat up from the darkest reaches of a nightmare. In that finite portion of a moment, Timmon Strongtail caught the tiniest gleam about the Sky-Skinner, beneath the mizzenmast, near the ship's wheel, and among a crowd of scurrying hurried creatures of all shapes and sizes and colors but who were unmistakably evil in the way the slunk and gibbered. There on the deck stood a figure as tall and menacing as he was hollow, like a cage of black ribs devoid of any inside, any heart or lungs or gut or even something vaguely resembling a soul. He was little more a creature than he was a form, a fleeting glimpse of imagination gone wrong, a travesty swathed in the skin of another. The great pelt of an arctic bear he wore about his shoulders like a shroud; its empty head and face devoid of a lower jaw hung limp over the Wolf's shoulder. His arms and legs were long and spidery, jointed, it seemed, in too many places, they twitched and spasmed motion rather than moving fluidly and with firm intent as any creatures should; and they were as four independent limbs rather than the appendages of a single being. The Wolf's ears were tattered flaps of skin that pointed straight toward the sky and more resembled a pair of spiked horns than anything a creature might use to listen. A crescent-moon smile of yellow teeth so soiled they were almost golden-brown, dripping slicks of froth down its breast spread over the face of the Wolf; and his single eye, like a white star in the blackest night, shone out over the distance between the two ships. The White-Eyed Wolf threw his head back and howled.

"Howw-OOOOOOOOO-A-ROOOOOOOOOOWWW!"

Stern and stoic, Timmon shouted to his crew on the deck, "Into their deck! Fire the harpoons! Take off their sails!"

"Why did the eagles leave the Valleys, grandfather?"

"No one knows, Tim. They left a long time ago for the lifting of warmer winds, all save one."

"Who was he, was he a great warrior, grandfather?"

"He was the truest and greatest of them all. He never abandoned his post as was his creed. His name was Prettle. Prettle Snowhelm was a true warrior. When all of the eagles left, he stayed alone and kept the skies as safe as he could."

"What happened to him, grandfather?"

"He was felled, finally, at the last stand."

"The last stand?"

"That's what we called our final battle, Tim. Prettle gathered the last free airships in the skies and united us all under a single banner. We took down our multicolored sails and brazen banners and replaced every bit of cloth with brilliant green, and at the top of every mast and the prow of every ship fluttered a single eagle's feather. Under the command of the ancient and wise commander, Wattle Featherscarf, the Greenfleet took the skies. We fought as long and as hard as we could. Our last battle, our last stand against the evil, the White-Eyed Wolf that had taken the skies, saw many of our heroes fall. Prettle among them."

"Is that when you were hurt, grandfather?"

"Indeed, and I would have died that day, but Prettle, my good friend, saved my life. While he leaned over me on the deck of that ship and cared for me I grasped his feathers in pain. He stood to return to the battle, and I had a feeling, Tim, a feeling that he would not return to me, that something terrible would happen if he left me there. I grabbed at his feathers, begging him to stay, trying to hold him back. But he was a true buccaneer, a peacekeeper, and a battle-worn soldier; he fought against my grip and left me there, bandaged and recovering as best I could. I had managed to rip a single feather free from him while I struggled to keep him from leaving. Then . . ."

"What happened then?"

"He fought the Wolf, and he . . . he lost. He fell from the deck a broken thing. I never saw him again. I left that ship that day, when we returned, beaten, and broken to the ground, and came home to you, my boy, to care for you and protect you. You're of me, Tim, and I knew that I needed to teach you what I could, help you learn, and help you find your own path whatever it may be."

"I want to be a buccaneer, grandfather! I'll avenge you, and the warrior, Snowhelm, and all the others who fought with you!"

"That's just it, lad. I want you to understand that way of life is not all songs and stories of heroism. There is a dark side to every moon, and there is danger in every adventure, and sometimes the danger is too much for one otter. I only want you to consider a life of peace; forget this fight and live your life in solitude. Meet a nice lass, have pups of your own, this is not your fight."

"I thought you once told me that freedom was everyone's fight?"

"I did."

"Grandfather?"

"Yes, my son?"

"What happened to that feather, the warrior Snowhelm's feather that you plucked from him before he fell?"

"You wear it above your eyes, lad. Keep his feather in your sights and me near your heart."

Like thunder cracks, the harpoons of the Summerswill split deckboards and railing into the Sky-Skinner, sending up showers of black splinters. Their trailing towlines whistled over the gap between the twin ships, their coils diminishing exponentially as more and more cord spun out into the sky until a searing moment when not cord remained, and every line went taut with a creak and a snap. The Summerswill listed to one side with the tension and the weight behind the Sky-Skinner.

"Bring us forward, full speed, Admiral!" Spittle flew from Timmon Strongtail's mouth with the force of his shout, and the admiral dutifully slammed his taloned foot into the accelerator. The Summerswill shot forward like a fired cannon-load, still dipping to her starboard with the attached tethers. As the lines bent and gave way, the Summerswill reared to her starboard, circling around behind the Sky-Skinner, on whose deck creatures raced back and forth with blades and pickaxes, attempting hurriedly to free the harpoons from their deck or to cut the lines that locked their ship to their enemy.

Within seconds the Summerswill had broken past the threshold of the Sky-Skinner's stern and was bringing up a wide arc around to the ship's port. The lines swept over the deck, tightly wound and swept those creatures too slow to avoid them off of their feet and flat on the deck. It only took a moment for the Wolf to realize what his rival captain was up to as he noticed the lines from the harpoons begin to stretch at angles against the masts of the Sky-Skinner's sails. With a guttural roar, something not unlike the sound of a nightmare given voice, he shouted to his crew,

"They're breaking the masts! Free those harpoons, you dolts!" When few creatures rushed to obey him and many and more fought to free themselves of the tow-lines or to find purchase on their now-listing deck, the White-Eyed Wolf made an example of the creature nearest him an unfortunate stoat. He slid his flaying knife from his belt beneath the massive arctic bear fur he wore about his body and lashed out with it so quickly the blade sang in the whipping wind and hissing rain. The stoat shrieked and reeled back, clutching his face where a slice of his cheek had just been removed as easily as a cook might dice a carrot. "Now." The immediate change of heart was astounding to the crew of the Summerswill, who watched from their own deck. The crew of the Sky-Skinner, driven by sheer terror and unwillingness to disappoint, lest they be carved as well, surged into action and went at the towlines and harpoons with a renewed fervor borne of the suffering of one of their own.

"Faster, Admiral!" Timmon was beside his first mate, fairly shouting in his ear, which was fortunately still covered by his great floppy hat. The Summerswill was fast turning in a tighter arc, and in a moment, if the masts of the Sky-Skinner did not snap, the Summerswill would collide with the much larger ship, ramming straight into it with their ironclad prow. This was a situation Timmon had not anticipated, and he had hoped simply to destroy the Sky-Skinner's maneuverability so that they might ram her many times over, gradually crippling the massive black galleon.

The Wolf, at his own helm, spread a grin of satisfaction. Spinning his wheel, he brought his own ship to her port, stretching the towlines ever tighter despite the protesting groans of his masts, which squealed and whined against the pressure. The first splinters erupted out of the bases of the Sky-Skinner's masts a heartbeat later as they began to separate from the deck, splitting like green branched up their middles with wooden screams. The Wolf had though, what he wanted, he was prow to prow with the catapulting Summerswill, and their collision was imminent. He would bring this fight to the decks of the ships, of that he was certain, and in the back of his mind, Timmon Strongtail knew it as well and gripped his blackwood staff tightly, gritting his teeth.

As if on cue, a storm of crows rose up from beneath both ships, a tornado mass of black feathers and screeching cries cutting swathes through the downpour of rain.

In that moment, Timmon and the Wolf locked eyes.

Then the twin ships crashed.

The sound of twin airships was deafening, punctuated by a resounding sphere of influential sound that rippled outward and, for a brief instant, stopped even the pouring rain and made the tempest's heart skip a beat. Timmon and his crew were cast forward, slamming with meaty thunks into the bulkheads, railings, and deck of the Summerswill. Cattatch alone had been in the air at the perfect moment and alighted onto the deck of the Summerswill, gazing out at the merged hulls of the two ships. The iron prow of the Summerswill had pierced deep into the hull of the Sky-Skinner; the two decks were almost on an even keel with one another, and the force of the propellers of each ship, now head-to-head, caused them to slowly turn, spiraling like an oak leaf in the torrential rain and lightning. Masts were split and cracked all around, and sails hung limp and sodden, collapsed over the decks in many places or billowing and flapping in the wind in no direction in particular. Both crews seemed to have been shook by the collision, and their was a brief time of quarter when both crews simply stared at one another, but it was Cattatch Dartwing who sounded the first battle cry, buckler and blade raised high in the air he called out to the sky above, below, and all around,

"Summerswill!" With that he cast himself at the enemy crew, flapping and hopping over the wreckage, fire in his eyes.

Timmon Stongtail lost no time in rousing his crew, taking a quick census and counting heads to ensure all were safe. Manica sleek with rain, cloak flying out behind him, hood down, and blackwood staff glowing bright gold, he launched himself off of the helm to the deck below, landing at a full sprint and scrambling over the impact point of the two ships and crashing headfirst into the fray, a battle growl surged from his lips, and he lashed out at the first foe to cross his path.

A great, burly, rancid-smelling raccoon loomed before Timmon. His face was hidden behind an iron mask, painted with a sneering toothy grin. Its shoulders and breast were plated in metal, and he brandished a thousand-times-nicked sabre that was brown with rust. The raccoon took immediate notice of the otter captain and surged over the wreckage, more like an amorphous monster than a creature. Its first cut was a hard downward arc that Timmon sidestepped easily, swinging out with his blackwood staff as he did; the blow caught the raccoon full in the face, but Timmon's foe was undeterred and shouldered his armored body into Timmon's, knocking him brutally to the deck. The raccoon stood over Timmon, eyes glittering with vicious intent. Remembering the blade at his side, Timmon, quick as a flash, unsheathed his cutlass and thrust upward into the raccoon's unarmored stomach. The beast looked downward through the eye slits in his mask and stared at the wound blossoming in his gut, locked eyes with Timmon once more, and then crashed unceremoniously to one side.

Standing, Timmon to a survey of the chaos and the carnage around him. Far to the port side of the Sky-Skinner, Neesa and Isaac had cornered a pair of roguish-looking stoats against the bulwark. The Summerswill crew lashed out with their rapiers while the stoats countered with a pair of wickedly spiked iron balls attached by chains to thick handles, swinging them back and forth and overhead in great downward swipes.

Cattatch and Hoory circled low over the tulmut, diving in assault at the few crows who dared part from their curtain of a thousand bodies that swirled around the battle, keeping the war being waged on the ship's decks at a ground level; the warriors of the Summerswill at least had nothing to fear from above.

Rigger had cocked a hand cannon into the crook of his shoulder and was holding off a proper band of miscreants and filth, firing into the crowd with reckless abandon such that none were enthused with the idea of pressing toward the front, lest they fall under Rigger's hapless crosshairs.

The massive figure of Mutter Stripeback, armored like a juggernaut and swinging his mace with grim precision cut a swathe through the crew of the Sky-Sinner, a veritable cloud of bodies surged around him, only to be cast back and into the air with every swing of his weapon. Trailing behind him a few paces, armored equally and lugging a repeating crossbow firing into the mass of enemy pirates, was Senna Stripeback, adding her iron-tipped bolts to the adrenalin-fueled fury of her son.

"But where was the Wolf?" Timmon wondered, spinning to survey the entire battlefield, "And where is the admiral?"

Through the gray clouds of rain, through the chaos of the battle, through the veil of scaled eyes, and through a shroud of disbelief, Timmon found the answer to his question. High atop the mast, along one of the boughs that supported the torn whipping sails of the Sky-Skinner, balanced precariously on uneasy and slick footing danced two gaunt figures. One was garbed in the old attire of an airship's captain, a great floppy hat slung low over his eyes, and a great beak protruding from beneath. The other was a massive hulk of sinew and ribcage; his hackles were raised and spiked like a line of horns down the spine of a creature brought forth from a terrible nightmare. The wolf gripped a small half-moon skinning blade in one long-fingered claw; his yellow frothing grin was a smile of more teeth than Timmon had ever seen in a single mouth, each was chipped and rotten and mossy with growths, and his slaver spilled from his carbuncled lips in torrents with the rain. His white eye was away from Tim, and he saw only the movements of the juggernaut through the movement of the bear skin atop its arched back, though he thought it to be speaking but above the din of the battle he could not be sure.

His thoughts and attention were cut short as Timmon spied the quick movements of a figure approaching him, a skittering figure, long and lean. A stoat garbed all in skins save a thick pair of iron pauldrons and a full helm, wielding a pair of wickedly curved figures. Its arms were already cut a dozen times from close combat, and the thing snickered a sharp laugh that echoed beneath his helm to form a chorus of gay jubilee like nothing Timmon had heard before. The Laugher cut a swathe through the chaos of the battle, the golden glow from Timmon's staff gleaming like fire in its black eyes reflected through the frog-slit in his helmet.

With lithe tenacity, the Laugher shoved his way forward, barred only for a moment by Cattatch who dove from above, swinging a sling laden with stones in a tight whirl above his skull-capped head. The Laugher did not hesitate and barely looked at his oncoming attacker; he merely bull rushed his shoulder toward the smaller bird and threw his breast into the shove; Cattatch bumbled over the stoat's pauldron and behind him, back into the fray.

"He-he-he-he-he-ha-ha-ha-ha-HA-HA-HA-HAHAHAHAHA!" The Laugher feigned a turn, lashing out at the downed songbird with one of his knives; it was enough to stir Timmon Strongtail into action. Before he could think, Timmon charged forward, swinging his staff in a wide arc at the stoat's helmed skull. There was no force of contact, and the blow threw Timmon off balance, so much that he barely caught himself before he fell. The Laugher had ducked the blow swiftly and easily and, with a single fluid movement, brought himself next to Timmon, so near that Timmon could feel the puffs of breath on his cheek as the Laugher cackled.

A piercing white pain shot down Timmon's left arm, and a crescent appeared in his skin where the Laugher had cut him. Before he could retort with a blow, the Laugher melted easily backward toward the fray, lashing out once more with his knives to put Timmon on his guard before he slid back into the crowd like a ghost among headstones.

With no time to meditate on his encounter, Timmon soon found himself back to back with a massive figure, the simple size of the bulk of muscle and roped sinew that had nudged into him threw Timmon into an immediate state of panic, and he whirled at the exact moment that Mutter Stripeback did. Both had weapons raised, staff against mace, though each stopped before a blow was struck.

"Cap'n!"

"Mutter! Where are the others?" Timmon searched the connected decks once again, straining for any sign of his crew and caught only flashes and instants of motion from his own warriors, who seemed as drowning swimmers beneath a sea of skins and dark iron-plated pirates.

The badger, much taller than his captain, spun all around, taking a swift survey of the decks.

"They're all here 'r there, Cap'n. 'Cept the adm'ral, I don' see him."

"He was up in the rigging with the Wolf, Mutter. Help me find them both, please!"

"Righ' on it, Cap'n!" With a lurching shift of his armored bulk, Mutter lifted his massive mace above his head and strode forward as easily as he might have waded through tall grass. A foolish fox turned to face him, sword and shield up, and only managed a small sound of fright and a rapid widening of his eyes before Mutter's mace crashed down upon his head, burying him into the deck beneath his feet. What was left of the enemy, Timmon could hardly look at.

A few steps at a time, Timmon followed in the wake left behind by the massive badger, lifting sword or staff only a handful of times to face a wayward foe, and then only to distract them for a moment while Mutter readied his mace for another blow before he struck down his captain's attacker.

Timmon noticed presently that any flesh showing through Mutter's plated armor was already crisscrossed on every inch with weeping wounds, cuts piling up on the patchwork of scars that had already covered him head to toe when Timmon had first met him. He was in awe for a moment at the true power and heart of the warrior before him, this umber-hulk of a creature that stood beside him, or in front of him, rather, in battle, and he was glad to have such a juggernaut on his side.

One step, then two, and a third, and fourth, and they found themselves below the bulkhead of the Sky-Skinner. Above them, the ship's tattered sails flapped and slapped one another soddenly and with bullwhip cracks, echoed only by the booming thunder and split forks of purple lightning that had begun to violate the storm. Even the murder of crows had grown closer to the fray in lieu of flying through the great epic storm that had formed all around the twin ships, diving and shrieking at the carnage that was growing on the decks below. Timmon took a small hop and a skip and managed to grab the railing of the helm above his head; muscles tensed and hood drawn back for a better look, he screened the deck while pulling himself up. The tide of the battle seemed to have turned, and the buccaneers of the Summerswill had begun to rout the undesirables of the Sky-Skinner. Neesa, Cattatch, Hoory, and Rigger stood back to back in a tight circle, lashing out at any creature that came near and doing a fair job of making sure that no enemies advanced toward the Summerswill's deck. Brattleby was threatening a group of pirates with a massive pot of bubbling, boiling oil, kept safe himself by his thick oven mitts, and Norrey and Isaac were tenderly tiptoeing about the deck, finishing off any enemies who had not yet given up, though hiding behind their blades like true soldiers lest any enemy surprise them or catch them off guard.

At that moment, a hatch opened beneath the fallen, shoving the offal of battle aside, and the admiral thrust his wobbly neck above the wooden plane of the warped and shattered deck, a massive grin shepherding itself across his beak.

"Admiral!" Timmon called.

"Aye, lad. I live, lost the Wolf though, looks though thin's been goin' well on your end!" Wattle Featherscarf pulled himself wholly up onto the deck, and it was clear he had fought valiantly. A large section of his great floppy hat had been sheared off, presumably by a razor-sharp skinning knife, and a good number of his feathers were missing or broken, but all in all, Timmon thought he looked in good health and in better spirits. Only Mutter broke the silence with a simple sentence, uttering what Timmon had feared since the beginning.

"Where's my mom?"

No life glittered in Senna Stripeback's eyes when the Wolf and the Laugher emerged from the fidgeting crowd of undesirables at the other end of the deck and shoved her limp form down on the deck. Her head lolled to one side, and Timmon could see where her life had left her.

The tensing of every muscle in Mutter Stripeback's massive form could be felt across the decks of both ships, like a breath of pressure before a pouring rain. His armor rattled as his arms and chest and legs and thick neck began to tremble in rage, and with a scream of deepest agony, he raised his mace and rushed forward.

Before Timmon could stop a thing and before he could take stock of what had happened, it was over.

Undesirables of every shape and size rushed forward, and the crew of the Summerswill, dumbfounded, were simply too slow to stop or interfere with what happened; they swarmed over Mutter, dozens of them at a time, covering him like ants over spilled sugar; though he would throw off a number in a moment, more still replaced them, and for every one he felled with a swipe of a paw or a blow from his mace, two took its place until there was only a shifting heaving mound of creatures scrambling over the downed form of Timmon's crew member and friend.

Casually, and not without a hint of arrogant presumption, the White-Eyed Wolf strode forward, and with a wave of one long-fingered claw, the mass of enemies sloughed off of Mutter who lay panting and tragically wounded on the deck. Timmon heard the Wolf speak, a mere whisper, something barely audible, but somehow deafening in the silence as all strained to hear his words. His tongue slithered over his yellow teeth like a snake's hiss, and his single eye never blinked and so rapt was Captain Strongtail that he missed completely what the Wolf had began to say,

"Do we have a deal?"

"What? Uh, no. Leave him be!" Timmon stamped the butt of his staff on the deck, letting out a thick thundering resonance and a flashing glow of gold like a miniature sun.

"Heh, heh, heh . . . the pup toys at parlay as a lass at a tea party. This is larger than you."

"I'll not treat with the likes of you, monster." Timmon noticed then that his crew had assembled behind him, a small formation of brothers and sisters in arms before a massive infantry of horrible creatures amid a swirling chaos of shrieking black birds.

The Laugher chuckled from behind his captain, and the echoed glee reverberated across the deck, and the whole world was laughing at Timmon Strongtail.

Timmon stretched that moment into a hundred years. He saw himself when he was young, playing at swords with sticks among ancient trees that had seen the world grow and blossom and might just live long enough to watch the worlds end if such an end was ever allowed to take hold. He saw the life of his grandfather and all he had done, and all the things he had shown him, both through his stories and through the love imbued within Timmon's blackwood staff; he saw his mother and his father who had never felt just right, like puzzle pieces in his life that were forced into place and didn't quite fit but were still the completion of a grand picture; and he saw the hearts and minds and beliefs of the crew at his back, the hope and the passion and the camaraderie. The was honor there, yes, but beneath the honor, beneath the pride and the sense of brotherhood and their loyalty to him, and beneath every infinite particle of what they were and represented and knew and thought and saw and were was something so simple and yet so all-encompassing that Timmon shed a tear . . .

. . . there was love there. Nothing much else, but love.

"Stand down, Wolf. Give my crew their lives. Let them leave in peace and I shall let yours do the same. Your murder, your pirates, your skinners, and all of the rabble that follows your crumb-trail of stink, hoping for a single glimpse at the power you claim to wield to bring them doggedly together. We let each other's followers go home, to their kin, to their kith, to the ones they care for and treasure. No tricks, no traps, and no quarter."

"No quarter, eh? You and I then?"

"You and I. We finish this, tonight. Now." With a furious battle cry, Timmon Strongtail rushed forward at his adversary at his darkest dreams.

"There is never any rush to grow up, Tim. Growing up and growing old come together, and if you're in any rush to grow up, it's only a matter of time before you begin to grow old. The heart and mind and spirit of being young is something we never cherish when we are young; it is fleeting, and when the day comes that we realize that those days have passed us by, there will always be an insatiable yearning to return to them. I don't ever want you to grow old, Tim, and when you do, I hope your heart remains young, and you remember all that I've taught you."

"I promise, grandfather."

"Do not promise, Tim. Never make a promise you are not certain to keep. Sometimes a moment will catch up with you, a moment you haven't the ability to stop, and in this moment you will be presented with a circumstance that will help you grow, whether you wish to or not. When this happens, you musn't fight these moments, but, rather embrace them. Just never forget who you are and who you were just a moment before."

In that moment, there were only Timmon Strongtail and Garrous Gerrmane, the White-Eyed Wolf. It was as though the storm of crows and the tempest of sheeting rain and splintering lightning had ceased to exist. No crews stood at opposite ends of the ship's decks; there was no detritus of battle underfoot; there were neither cries nor screams; there was no time.

Timmon was scarcely aware of casting off his cloak midsprint, nor was he conscious of the way he ran toward a small outcrop in the wreckage of the twin ships, sprinted to its apex and leaped into the air, bringing his blackwood staff behind his head with both paws clenched tight around its haft, his knuckles white with tension. Ready for a blow, the staff began to beam with light, piercing golden and yellow streams of incandescence poured forth from the shaft of Timmon's staff, so much so that crew members on both sides of the fray hid and shielded their eyes.

Beneath the shining star of Timmon's staff, the White-Eyed Wolf was an epiphany of shadow, his fur and heart and everything, he was the very deepest dark, so obsidian that the light from Timmon's staff seemed only to be eaten by the maw that he was.

The finality of the blow was cut short by the block that the Wolf cut with his half-moon skinning knife. The razor's edge cut into the shaft of Timmon's staff deeply, and for a moment, the light in the blackwood guttered as if all the power it possessed had been cut down with a single-shaved stroke . . .

.

.

.

. . . then the light burst forth like a grassfire, spinning out and out in a spiral torrent that spilled echoing light of every color imaginable across the decks.

Garrous Gerrmane faltered backward, and Timmon surged forward on the assault. He struck out high at the Wolf, a blow caught by the Wolf's blade with a chuk of metal into wood. The Wolf twisted his blade with a crescent moon sneer and ripped Timmon's staff to his left, forcing him to follow the pull lest the staff be wrenched from his grip.

Rolling with the counter, Timmon spun off of his heel and ripped his staff free of the Wolf's blade, switching its grasp to one paw; he tore his cutlass from its place in his belt and lashed out a high arcing cut at the Wolf's face, one which his adversary easily backstepped.

Timmon knew in an instant that his feint had worked and struck out low with his other weapon, his blackwood staff catching the Wolf in the crook of his knee with a snapping sound.

But the Wolf was no fool as his knee bent out from under him, he lunged forward with his good leg, foot planted firmly and closed the distance between him and Timmon Strongtail, tackling him to the deck.

Over and over the two combatants rolled, neither losing his grip on his weapon; Timmon braced his blackwood staff between him and the Wolf, his cutlass dropped and forgotten while the Wolf pressed his skinning knife closer and closer to Timmon's face, its blade gleaming and wet in the lightning.

With a great surge of force, Timmon punched outward with both fists, bringing the shaft of blackwood into contact with the Wolf's long snarling nose with a gratifying crunch. Spinning overtop of his foe, Timmon brought his staff back for a strong blow, exposing his body foolishly. Garrous Gerrmane, the White-Eyed Wolf, took his opportunity and snapped upward with his jaws wide, with less than a moment's notice. Timmon let go of his staff with one hand and brought his manica down to guard his throat and exposed stomach. The Wolf's jaws closed around the overlapping iron and bore down with all the force of a sprung trap. Tooth and metal cracked and bent, and dozens of dents forced themselves within, biting down on the flesh of Timmon's arm within his armor. Gritting his teeth, Timmon bit back a cry of pain for a span of seconds, but as the Wolf closed down harder and harder, he let the exclamation escape his lips, and he helplessly rolled to his back once more.

His feet back under him, one leg crooked with cracked bone, the Wolf arched his great spine over, standing but never letting his jaws leave his preys arm and tightened every muscle he could muster, splitting enamel and popping iron rivets from their fastenings as he did so, crushing Timmon's flesh within his own protective sleeve as he did so. Growling through closing teeth, he addressed his enemy,

"Is this your all, otter? Is this what your father prepared you for? I'll set your skin as my cabin rug."

Blinded with pain, Timmon could not believe his eyes as the White-Eyed Wolf sprouted a pair of great dark wings, broken as one appeared. It was only a moment before Timmon realized the wings were not his own, and faster and faster the massive span of the feathers grew as if rushing at the deck from some dream or hope or wish from beyond possibility. It's a mirage, a trick of the rain through the fire and the squalls, through the chaos of battle, Timmon thought. Then a sound pierced the night, a sound not heard echoing in the darkness of the Valleys for some time, a piercing and lilting cry that perforated the ears of each and every member of both crews, and a great many creatures down below, witnessing the battle on high from the safety of the ground. It was not until Timmon heard the cry that he dared hope . . .

"Keeeeeeeeeeeeeeeeee-EEEEEEEEEEEERRRRRRRRRRRRRRRRRRRR!"

The force of the blow to the Wolf's back tore Timmon with it, and only as the Wolf's jaws opened in surprise was he released, slammed into the railing of the Sky-Skinner. His back alight with pain but alive. He managed a glance over his shoulder, only to see the last traces of the White-Eyed Wolf plummeting into the nothingness of the sky below amid a flurry of white and ebon-brown feathers, his final howl tearing a hole in the air around him, decreasing as he fell, his single eye glowing pale in the nothingness until he disappeared beneath the storm clouds.

"Howw-OOOOOOOOO-A-ROOOOOOOOOOWWW!"

The next minutes passed by for Timmon Strongtail like a blur, and when asked afterward, he could barely describe the details and was lost for all comment.

The crew of the Summerswill bound all of their captors and took their weapons with very little resistance; the enemy was stunned silent beyond words, and it was as though every ounce of fight that had been left in them had fallen away with their captain. One by one they were arrayed on the starboard side of the Sky-Skinner, their binds woven through the railing to keep them down. The crew of the Summerswill moved through their zombified and stupefied foes with little problem; only Mutter did not stray and knelt a silent vigil over the form of his mother, his massive form blocking the driving rain from marring her features any further.

Timmon wandered somewhat aimlessly, he pulled his cloak tightly around his shoulders and cowled his hood low over his eyes, holding the soft glow of his blackwood staff against his chest. Dark shapes seemed to move around him, circling like carrion birds, even minutes after the murder of crows had followed their fallen captain to the ground to circle above his grave.

Across the ship, a single form sobbed, a strange sight giving that it was from the hulking form of a battle-worn raccoon clad all in iron and fur. Timmon approached this form and said nothing, only looked out from under the edge of his hood, his face underlit by the glow from his staff; and for once, Timmon looked a terrifying figure. The raccoon looked up, and from beneath his face, Timmon could see where his wound gaped across his neck and down the top of his breast; he was dying, and there were tears in his eyes.

"Why do you cry?" Timmon asked.

"Die? You will not die while I command your ship."

"You'll execute a lot of us." The raccoon's retort was sharp and filled with acid.

"I am not going to execute you, you won't die."

"Be that as it may. You already have. I'll not live past this last flight."

"Who?"

"My son, Nikkin, do the least and tell him his father loved him." The raccoon bowed his head, and with final gurgling sob, what was left of his life drained away.

Timmon broke down then, knelt on the deck, and wept.

"Are you hurt, my gracious captain?" Hoory, feathers still ruffled from combat and a crack in his monocle, bent down over his captain and inspected him. "You've many cuts and scrapes here, looks as though you gave our vagabond enemy a tumultuous what for, eh?"

"I didn't, Hoory. I was barely a part of the battle at all."

"I do beg to differ, last I saw, you and the mighty Mutter were cutting a swathe through the enemy as if you a pair of dull knives through melting butter, as it were. Here, let me tend to you, then you can go about your captainlike duties."

Captain Strongtail stood patiently while his medical officer debrided his wounds and applied poultices and linen wraps to them all. His manica was stripped off tenderly, exposing the wrecked skin beneath, which Hoory took great care to bandage under great pressure and with a soothing balm of mint and red basil. Timmon had not noticed during the battle, but he was indeed quite the wounded mess. A score of weeping cuts crisscrossed his arms and chest, and along the midline of his brow, he had a grazing cut that was none too deep; but Timmon surmised that if he had been less vigilant or had the instinct to move only an instant later, such a thing might have been a fatal blow.

"You had a close shave here, lad."

"I can see that, Hoory, though I can scarcely remember when that cut came or who dealt the blow."

"Such is the fervor of a creature in combat, the strive to save our own lives oft drives us to move without thinking."

"But why me, Hoory? When so many others have—" Timmon did not finish his thought; instead he turned his head and found himself staring at the gaunt figure of Mutter Stripeback, back arched over his mother and motionless, like a mournful grotesque keeping a stone vigil.

"That is the nature of battle, Tim, of war. We fight for what we believe in whether it be for good or ill. Even these vanquished foes bound to the railing behind us, they truly believed in what they were doing or were so terrified of their master that their fear and their loathing became a true travesty of faith. There is no doubt in my mind, lad, that our mission was a solemn quest for the greater good. Ours, like many before, has not come without its consequences, its costs. In the end though, what we have done is right, I believe it." Hoory looked Timmon in the eyes, bending his head as it was necessary and held his gaze for several moments. He spoke nothing further but only met Timmon's eyes with his own great molten-gold ones, then took his leave, ambling across the deck in search of other creatures in need of any medical care, both friend and foe alike.

Timmon stood fully bandaged and gathered his manica up under the crook of his wounded arm. It was only a moment in the dying rain before Cattatch, Rigger, and the admiral emerged from beyond the veil that Timmon's eyes had begun to cast over the world. All three stood stoic like statues, saluted, and then set in on him.

"Congratulations, Cap'n, we did well today, didn't we? Wolf's gone, he's gone!" Cattatch bounced happily, half-helm clanking back and forth on his dome-shaped head.

"Yes, Cattatch, you did admirably; without you to lead the charge I fear we may have been the defenders in that melee and not the aggressors." Timmon spoke almost from beyond himself, saying what he knew he had to say and what he did believe, for the songbird had been a veritable berserker during the conflict, but his mind was still overrun with the suddenness of which it had ended and the ghastliness of battle's aftermath.

"Cap'n, what're we to do with the pris'ners? We can't kill 'em, can we? That wouldn't be right. Would it?" Rigger glanced furtively around as though the prisoners may be listening to his comments, and indeed, some of the nearby undesirables were craning their necks and ears in order to discover their fate.

"Of course not, Rigger. We'll take them belowdecks, bound and gagged and go to ground; from there we lead them out, leave them all bound, save one, let that one unbind his mates through the day; by then we'll be far and away to the north to find our own kin." Timmon's mind then was a flurry of images, visages of his parents and his grandfather, lost and alone deep within the White-Eyed Wolf's mines, backs breaking under the cruel whips of his cohorts.

"Good plan, Cap'n!" Rigger trotted off to relay the news to the remainder of the crew who stood watch over their captives or worked to clear the debris from around the point where the twin ships had collided, which, thankfully, was turning out to be a task in the favor of the Summerswill whose iron prow had sustained little damage in the crash, thanks to Mutter Stripeback's superb craftsmanship.

"'N the Sky-Skinner, lad?" the admiral grumbled.

"We set her afire, Admiral. There's naught else to do. The Wolf is gone; his crew is ours; we do what's right from here on out, but this ship shall never fly again."

"Well spoken, lad. There's a creature missin' from the captives though." The admiral's eyes shifted over their prisoners from beneath his great floppy hat, which was none the worse for wear despite the slice that had been taken out of it; it had returned to its old amorphous shape.

"Who?" Timmon quickly scanned the enemy furtively, though he quickly realized the futility of this as he did not know each of them by sight, and many of them wore masks.

"That laughin' stoat. He ain't nowhere to be seen. Been through the entire ship, not hide nor hair o' him."

"The Laugher."

"Tha's what you been callin' him? Suiting name I suppose, but no, he ain't here, lad."

"A pity."

"Don' seem too broken up lad, you alrigh' with the fact he's free?"

"No. But I knew that this conflict wasn't over, Admiral. If he is aboard, he'll die with his ship. If not, then I am glad he fell in battle. He was something different, Admiral. All of the others, they were soldiers, undesirables, but still just foot creatures under the Wolf. That one was different. I could feel it in him. I could see it in those eyes."

"Only a mad creature takes glee from battle."

"Then he was mad, and this world is better rid of him. Come, Admiral, have our crew take the prisoners belowdecks and have Brattleby bring up one of his pots of oil and splay it o'er the deck of the Sky-Skinner. When we pull away, have Rigger fire that hand cannon he's so good with into the Skinner's deck. That should set her afire. From there it's straight to the ground, and we set the undesirable crew free, and we take to the north to do what we really came here to do. I'm going to the helm. Once all of that is complete, holler up, and we'll be rid of this thing that they call a ship."

"Aye, aye to all that, Cap'n. Yer' father would be proud."

"I don't know as he would be. He never wanted this life for me."

"Didn't he. Lad, I found this after the Wolf fell, best I can figger, it belongs to 'ya." From within his gray admiral's jacket, Wattle Featherscarf fished out what Timmon could hardly believe was truly there, and as if on cue, its sister feather fluttered from Timmon's brow into his eyes, and the two were perfect dopplegangers, save that both were real.

The admiral, Wattle Featherscarf, held a long pristine white feather, the perfect twin to the one that had been woven in Timmon's fur since he was but a pup.

Timmon had scarcely believed until this moment, but there it was in front of him—an eagle feather.

It took them several hours to move the crew of the Sky-Skinner to the brig in the lowest reaches of the Summerswill and less than a few minutes to spread Brattleby's cooking oil over the deck and the halls beneath the black frigate. None of the crew of the Summerswill had any interest in delving beneath the first deck of the Sky-Skinner, the further they walked through its rooms and halls, the more disgusted and mortified they became. Every corner and every wall was amass with grisly symbols painted in things that they could not believe, and the floors and walls were carpeted and walled with skins of every description. Beaded doorways were found at closer inspection to be decorated with the minute bones of many creature's paws and feet and the stench that permeated every inch of the ship and stuck in their nostrils like pine sap drove them to nausea.

Backing the Summerswill from where her iron prow had lodged itself in the hull of the Sky-Skinner, Timmon Strongtail called from the helm, "Now, Rigger!"

There was a single powder shot, followed by a boom of heat, a resounding wave of flames that spread so quickly that for a moment the black ribcage of the Sky-Skinner was alight in every shade of orange, red, yellow, and liquid blue. The crew of the Summerswill watched from the safety of their own deck for near an hour until the skeletal mass of the Sky-Skinner's silverstone core fell from the smoldering hulk like the veins of a leaf cast from a wing caught in a forest fire, plummeting to the ground far below with a whistling scream to where it finally fell to rest.

No one marked their location at that exact moment, as no one was interested in remembering where the Sky-Skinner was finally laid to rest.

When that was finished, Timmon Strongtail ordered the Summerswill to the ground. The ship landed among a stretch of brush somewhere in the center of the badlands, still east of the Mane. One by one, the captives from the Sky-Skinner were led from the Summerswill and ordered to sit. Still shocked or perhaps resigned to their fate, they obeyed, though many without some grumbling and muttered curses. By the time many more hours had elapsed, what remained of the crew of the Sky-Skinner sat assembled in the dirt, Isaac cut the bonds of a one-eyed rat and waddled back aboard the ship, which rose aloft into the skies and to the north and east before the rat had even begun to free his compatriots.

"Where to now, Captain?"

"The mines, forward."

It took nearly a day for the Summerswill to reach the Wolf's mine beneath the mountains of the Mane. Every crew member was once again ready for battle, strapped in all armor with their weapons ready as the Summerswill alighted over the hollow in the mountain's foothills where the entrance to the mines lay. To all of their surprise, they found the entrance, a great door formed by a leviathan trilithon of stones, deserted of undesirables.

Without a moment's hesitation, Timmon Strongtail, blackwood staff raised high above his head, cutlass in the other paw, and mangled manica back in place, shouted to his crew and was swallowed by the dark maw of the mines, trailed by his trusted friends.

What they found beneath the mountains was something that none of them ever spoke of again. Hundreds of creatures of every kind had been left behind, bound in chains, when the undesirables had left, presumably when the Crag fell, though none could be sure, crew member or enslaved, as no time passed beneath the mountain where it was always darkest. Furtively searching, cutlass now sheathed and staff high above his head to shine light, Timmon looked for his family. When he came upon a bound group of pitiful creatures, he would smash their bindings with the butt of his staff for a great majority of them were poorly fashioned and badly rusted things.

"Go! Go to the surface, my ship is there! My crew will have food, water! Go! Now!" Timmon shouted at them, tears welling in his eyes with every word, for the more he searched, the farther he seemed from finding his family.

Little by little the slaves of the White-Eyed Wolf's iron mines trickled into the daylight where it became wholly apparent to the crew of the Summerswill what they had been through. Their bones fairly erupted from their skin with malnutrition, and their eyes were dry with dehydration. They shielded their eyes from the noonday sun, and a great many of them cast themselves to the dirt before their saviors, weeping openly and hugging their feet, exhausted, afraid, beleaguered, but free.

Brattleby, Rigger, and Neesa ran among them, passing out ladles of water and bits and pieces of hard bread and bowls of leek and lentil soup while Hoory and Cattatch moved through the masses, aiding where they could. All had slack looks on their faces, something apart from pity and far from sadness, closest maybe to disbelief. Disbelief that any creature could do anything like this; it was madness, but it solidified in their minds that the crew of the Summerswill was on the right side of this war, the pleading eyes of those they had rescued put all of their doubt out of their minds.

Deep below, Timmon sprinted through the caverns and tunnels of the mine, tripping more than once over stray tools and overturned carts, now calling out at the top of his lungs, "Grandfather! Grandfather! Mother! Father! GRANDFATHERRR!"

Far away, Timmon heard a voice, choked and dry, barely a whisper, though to the owner, it was the best part of a shout, "Tim?"

There, betwixt a stand of stalagmites was the perfect arch of his parents, kneeling side by side, keeping a silent blind vigil over the gaunt form between them. It was not until Timmon saw the glint of light of his blackwood staff blink off of his grandfather's eyes that Timmon let himself be relieved.

He was alive . . .

◆ ◆ ◆ Barely.

"Grandfather, please! Hold on!" Kneeling over him, Timmon could see that the life had nearly left his eyes. He was thin, too weak to rise, and barely strong enough to smile, but smile he did.

"Tim. Little Tim, I knew you could do it. I knew it."

"Please . . . don't go." Timmon cried openly, tears soaking the fur on his face, glittering in the light from his blackwood staff, from his grandfather's blackwood staff.

"It's my time, lad. I've lived a long time, and it's your time now. Take care, be safe, and never forget everything I've taught you."

"I won't. I won't! I promise."

"Son, find the legacy. It's Sierra's, find it for me."

"The legacy? Grandfather, I don't know what you mean."

"Please, Tim. You need to know."

"I, I can't do it without you."

"You can, and you have."

"Wait! Please! I'll take you to the ship, we have medicine!"

"You are my medicine, Tim. You."

"Please."

"I love you, Tim."

"I love you too . . . Dad."

With that there was no more.

Timmon Strongtail emerged from the mine with his father's body in his arms, blackwood staff glowing brighter than it ever had before, such that the shadows cast by the noonday sun were blown opposite by its luminescence. He did not say a word, and he was followed closely by the two otters he had known his entire life—his mother and father. He simply boarded the Summerswill and went to the ship's lock room. There he wrapped his father's body in a blanket and engaged the lock when all of the creatures they had rescued were aboard.

Once aloft, in his cabin he was alone save the otters he had believed to be his mother and father. He stripped off his manica and unbuckled his cutlass; standing before his window, he watched the clouds pass by. He did not look to them as he spoke to them, fearing that they would see his tears.

"You knew?"

"We did, Timmon. I'm sorry for all of the pain this must cause, but your father was adamant that we continue the charade for fear of the Wolf."

"Why?"

"He thought that if the Wolf knew you were his son, he may come for you. He gave you to us when you were so small, just a bundle of fur in a blanket and told us to keep you safe. 'He's the one,' he said. 'He'll save us all in time.' We thought that he would never come back for you, so we raised you, but after a time, return he did. After that he was your grandfather, he wanted only to tell you stories and watch you grow."

"He wanted this for me? Why didn't he just say so?"

"He wanted you to find your own path, and if it never meant taking the skies, then that's what he wanted. He asked us to discourage you; he asked us to mark his stories false. When you saw through all of it and still wanted to venture out, I think he knew that you had finally found your path, and when you left, we knew that it was what he wanted."

"And when the Wolf came?"

"He took us in the night, while we all slept. Despite everything, despite the theater and the role-playing, he knew you were who you are. We did our best to keep your father safe, Tim, but he was old and so weak near the end. He always knew you'd come though. He kept saying, 'Timmon will come, my son will come,' even at the end. He waited for you in the end, but there was nothing left in him. We think he just wanted to say goodbye."

"And the legacy? What is it?"

"We don't know, Tim. Honestly, we do not know."

"Get out."

Out they went, and Timmon once more broke into tears, and this time he wasn't sure if he would ever stop.

Miter Strongtail was laid to rest by the water under a great oak tree just on the shore. Beside him was laid his old shipmate, Senna Stripeback. There was much weeping, but in the end, the crew of the Summerswill knew that the adventure they had set out on all that time ago had come full circle. The Wolf was dead. But full circle or no, the undesirables had not been vanquished, merely disbanded. There was chaos in the badlands as the warlords and chiefs vied for control of the mongrel hoards, and Timmon knew that their work was far from over.

There was still, also, the matter of his father's cryptic last words. The legacy, Sierra's legacy. Timmon had spent many nights scouring the ancient captain's logs of Sierra Riverrush, finding only flight logs, crew reports, cargo manifests, and the odd anecdote.

Timmon knew it was in there somewhere though, though what it was, he was not sure. He resolved to figure it out sooner or later, he must, for his father.

Sitting beneath the oak tree by the side of one of the rivers of the Valleys in the land of Sylva, Timmon stared at his father's grave, missing him, loving him, and wondering. To the east, the otters who had masqueraded as his parents sailed their longboat out of his life and into memory. Though he loved them still, Timmon wanted them to go about their own lives, to leave him to his father's fight, to his fight. They need not be involved; they need not be in danger for his sake, not anymore.

"Cap'n?" Wattle Featherscarf ambled over, crutching himself with his taproot walking stick, eyes hidden under his great floppy hat.

"My good captain." Hoory had come over as well. "Where are we bound?"

Timmon shut his eyes for a moment and brought a paw to his brow, running both eagle feathers through his palm, feeling the silky way they slid through his grasp, the way they knew him, the way they knew the way.

"We're going up. Higher than before. Higher than ever."

The End

Brothers Malloy
NJ USA
2012